Praise for
CLONEDROID THE NEW WAVE

"**Clonedroid: The New Wave...has excellent tension and a big crunchy question to engage readers...**"
~**Tor.com**

"Cate Bronson has done a fine job crafting accessibility in a plot... Abe's point of view is by far the most vivid stance for the story and most entertaining...and the plot rewards those who pay careful attention from the start..."
~*Writer's Digest*

"It's the kind of thing that Robin Cook has in his books...It is classic hard sci-fi and it's a wonderful book. I'm telling you, Clonedroid is a thriller! You have to read it!"
~*Patzi Gil of Joy on Paper, a syndicated radio program*

"**Super fun hard sci-fi novella in the vein of Asimov and Heinlein. Page turner all the way through...I love that I couldn't predict the ending.**"
~***Chad Parsons, Award-winning Author***

"This novel kept me turning the pages...By the end of the book, I realized we only had a glimpse of this newly-imagined creature, and that left me wanting more..."
~*L.K. Simonds, Author of ALL IN*

"Bronson's clever, high-tech tale exposes a possible future where the fine line between human and A.I. is frighteningly thin. Clonedroid is a well-timed premonition and a warning, much like Ian Malcom's famous line from Jurassic Park."
~*Bria Burton, Award-winning Author*

"Fun read with a twist…If you enjoy near-future sci-fi and are looking for a relatively quick read, this should be on your list."
~*M.J. Carlson, Suspense Author*

"I found Clonedroid to be a suspenseful and exciting read. Now, to wait for the sequel."
~*Martin Von Cannon, Author*

"Wow… Clonedroid, The New wave is a highly creative, thoughtful, intelligent and carefully woven story that cannot be put down. I finished it in two nights and thought–this should be a movie!!"
~***Amazon Reader***

"Superb! One of the best sci-fi books I read in recent memory. The author has a great writing style… I sure hope there's a sequel this would be a great series."
~*Goodreads Reader*

"If you like Asimov and robots…"Abe" put me in mind of R. Daneel Olivaw of the Asimov novels…That is not a bad thing… Overall, this is a book for any sci fi lover, and I am certainly looking forward to the next book!!!!"
~*Amazon Reader*

"Fantastic new "classic" hard science fiction. Like Asimov's later writing in style, but with Crichton's technical detail. It even has the social commentary typical of classic sci fi, along with real science…I couldn't put it down and finished in one shot. Hopefully we see more of this."
~***Goodreads Reader***

"Great Read! CloneDroid is an incredible page-turner! I picked it up and couldn't put it down… Would make an excellent movie as we don't see the end coming until…well, the end! Can't wait to read more of her work."
~*Amazon Reader*

CATE BRONSON

CLONEDROID
THE NEW WAVE

This novel is a work of fiction. Names, characters, places, and incidents are the product of the author's imagination or are used fictitiously and are not to be construed as real. Any resemblance to actual persons, living or dead, events, locales, businesses, or organizations is entirely coincidental.

Copyright © 2019 by Catherine A. Infanti
Clonedroid: The New Wave
ISBN: 9781081916121

All rights reserved. No part of this story and publication may be reproduced or transmitted in any form or by any means whatsoever, electronic or mechanical, including photocopy, scanning, recording, or any information storage and retrieval system, without permission in writing from the author.

Book design by Catherine A. Infanti and Steven B. Infanti.

Front cover and eBook image design by Deb Von Cannon of Urban Artist Florida Studio

URBAN ARTIST FLORIDA STUDIO, LLC
www.urbanartistflorida.com
urbanartistflorida@gmail.com
941-527-7364

Independently published

Printed in the United States of America

For additional information, visit www.catebronson.com

For Steve

*"You can have no dominion greater
or less than that over yourself."*

— Leonardo da Vinci

1

Abe lay on his back in the darkened room, staring at the dead ceiling lights entombed overhead. He shivered. The temperature in the lab had dipped through the night thanks to corporate conservation efforts. The scrubs he wore provided little warmth, and wisps of fine body hair and goosebumps had risen in response. Rubbing his hands together to generate heat, Abe swiped them up and down both arms. It did nothing to ward off the chill surrounding him or the cold he felt deep inside as he lay stretched out, like a slab of meat, on a metal surface. The examination table remained his bed of choice. He preferred it to the cot in the corner. Its icy-hardness reminded him of who he was and what he would become. Abe needed that. He needed to avoid illusions of comfort. No room existed in his life for complacency. Not now. Not ever.

Complacency is death.

Abe listened to the sub-audible purr of a wall-encased timer as it ticked off seconds in precise increments. His internal computerized clock, accurate beyond a fraction of a nanosecond, also kept perfect time. It tracked each moment that propelled him forward toward the only thing that mattered—*life.*

…twenty-four hours zero minutes four seconds… three… two… one…

Abe closed his eyes.

He readied himself as the automated lights blazed to life at exactly six o'clock to hum irritatingly overhead. His eyelids fluttered open, almost mechanically. The glare from above stabbed his sensitive cobalt blue eyes. Lifting a hand to his face, Abe filtered the light through long fingers until his pupils adjusted, then lolling his head to one side, he let a mass of blond hair shield his face. Abe now focused on the door and ignored the blinding light overhead, the unforgiving metal beneath, and the mounting bitterness from within.

…twenty-three hours fifty-nine minutes thirty-six seconds… thirty-five… thirty-four…

Instinctively, his eyes scanned the lab door, not staring at it but visualizing the massive double doors beyond.

…thirty-two… thirty-one… thirty…

The gear mechanism turned and retracted, breaking the hermetic seal with a *washoomp*. Air forced itself from one chamber into the next and swept through the long corridor of unlocking doors. When the nearest doors opened, they produced a mechanical sound that could be heard by anyone in the lab. When the furthest doors unlocked, they generated a reverberation that only Abe detected from this distance.

Every morning, at precisely thirty seconds after the lights ramped on the doors leading to the lab opened. Security guards at Multipurpose Android and Cloning Corporation were expected to utilize this time to scrutinize all laboratories before the doors released. Virtual monitors shimmered before them to reveal anything sinister, giving guards the chance to override the process if necessary. With time, this safety measure and many others had fallen away. Guards had traded occupational obligation for the comfort of hot coffee and idle prattle with early-bird employees.

In the same mode, lab techs for the android division disregarded a few routine procedures, trudging into the lab without a second glance at their surroundings. And why not? MACC offered one of the most secure facilities in the world. What was the harm? What was there to notice? Nothing would be damaged. Nothing could get in or get out. Not microbes, not androids. Nothing existed here to trigger a lock-down. Even Abe gave no one a reason for concern. He was a passive, routine test subject, no more out of place than a microscope. Besides, MACC had sensitive devices staged in every corner of the building. A hint of anything out of place would trip alarms. As a result, the bleary-eyed zombies working here ignored protocol as they shuffled into the lab every morning. Passing Abe, they headed toward the steaming pot of coffee.

…twenty-three hours fifty-eight minutes fifty-five seconds… fifty-four… fifty-three…

The clock in his head kept perfect time as the droning whirr of a fan deep within the belly of the building redoubled. The sound echoed through the ventilation shafts. Abe had detected the change in tempo as the heater geared up to elevate the temperature to a respectable standard.

While one segment of his cybernetic brain surveyed his surroundings, other sectors dealt with additional tasks, such as preserving the countdown and focusing on complex web-based functions. And yet another sector of his fluid mind preoccupied itself with those nagging human-like thoughts that far too often plagued him.

The thought that commanded his attention most in recent days centered upon his purpose. His value to humanity had shifted from something remarkable and contributory to that of a piece of standard technology, valued more for the parts within than for the sum of the whole. Beyond that, his usefulness to MACC had ceased.

Abe's brow wrinkled.

No human deserves so little reverence as this.

His jaw muscles locked.

But, of course, I am not regarded as human.

Clonedroid: The New Wave

In the history of his making, and nearly overnight, the global populace had come to regard humanoid robots with tolerant indifference. Some cultures, like those of China, Japan, and Korea, even embraced artificially intelligent beings as human. But somehow, Abe had fallen short. He was different. Toward him, product development surveys around the world offered mixed reviews and a mash of emotions. Wariness ranked highest, and for a good reason. Abe was no ordinary android. In fact, he was not a robot at all. Possessing both living and artificial components, he represented something altogether different.

Known only as Prototype 2112, and christened "Abe" by lab techs, he was something that many consumers regarded as off-putting. In appearance, he too closely resembled a human. In functionality, he too closely resembled a robot, complete with a computerized brain. And as for his soul—well, most humans believed he possessed none. Regarded as an odd cybernetic hybrid, Abe was a product that offered something beyond standard robotics, and something beyond human. While his design and construction had made scientists and market speculators giddy, his completion had made the general populace uneasy. Instead of welcoming him into their world, humans had shunned the very idea of him and what he represented, fearing that which they did not understand. To best ease their consciences, they had, for the most part, dismissed him as a long-lasting, mechanized sack of blood and bones, and nothing more.

Abe's heart sank, and he swallowed back a wave of discontent. Lying motionless on his side, he continued to stare at the glass door, waiting for time to pass.

Perhaps, humans held a razor-thin right to their notions of him. To be fair, he had been genetically pieced together and lab-grown like Frankenstein's monster—a distasteful reference he tried to dismiss. Similarly, his creators refused to accept him and his true potential.

While Abe struggled to fathom *why*—creating him only to destroy him—he understood human apathy and the reason behind their disinterest and disregard toward him. It made their work and their lives easier—it made things comfortable.

Abe had learned early on that his presence, or even the knowledge of his existence, made most people uncomfortable. In his limited interaction with important guests from beyond the lab, he had detected hesitation in speech patterns and body language. They often tried to conceal it, but their denial was another coping mechanism against fear. He posed no visible threat, yet people feared him all the same. Deep down, at some level, they all knew what he represented. He was a reminder to them of their greed, guilt, ambitions, and ignorance. He reminded them that playing god (when one is not a god) has only one outcome, one that does not end well. Abe was that outcome—the result of taking a good idea much too far.

And then there was a small segment of the population, like those who owned and directed MACC, who were not fearful of him or anything for that matter. They remained purposeful and deliberate in their callousness. He also knew the reason behind their motivations and malevolence. In their arrogance, they had never attempted to conceal it. To them, he was less than human, less than a lab animal, and more disposable than the dogs, cats, mice, and monkeys once caged here and tortured to death in experiments. Abe meant even less to these people than a "tin-can man." He was valued only as a commodity, a number on a balance sheet, a means to an end and nothing more. They were ungrateful, considering how extensively he had contributed to the advancement of science and their careers, but that was life and death in the human world.

Having served his purpose as a high-end product of innovation, Abe knew all too well that he now sat in the lab fully depreciated. Nothing remained of Prototype 2112 on paper, except for a business write-off. Downgraded, he would soon face his final, fatal purpose. To salve consciences, corporate heads spoke openly to one another about it, as if they had already disposed of him. But none of that mattered. Only the countdown mattered.

Timing is everything.

A hint of a mocking smile appeared on his lips.

…twenty-three hours fifty-seven minutes forty-eight seconds… forty-seven… forty-six…

Abe sat up. Using his arms to brace his body, he repositioned himself sideways to the length of the examination table, letting his legs dangle over the edge like a patient waiting in a doctor's office. He stared across the bright room at the coffee maker on the counter as it sputtered into action and gurgled away, its internal clock out of sync by two minutes and fourteen seconds with the wall timer. By the time the first drops of water drained through the roasted granules, the bitter-rich scent would have already reached him. Its pleasantness had long ago lost any appeal. The vapors would soon billow from the brewing machine en mass, waft through the ventilated air stream, and deliver an overpowering odor to his sensitive nostrils until his stomach churned. It was a daily occurrence he had learned to live with, given that he had little choice. Abe had often envisioned smashing the machine to bits. But he preferred sleeping on the stone-cold table to being caged every night, so he had tamed his outrage early on. His relative freedom in the lab remained a direct result of strict obedience and cooperation. Loyalty to the firm had its privileges, even if they were few. Not one employee, not even Tamera—the project leader and the closest thing he had to a friend—would blink twice about having him tethered to the table if he gave them a reason. Had Abe possessed an "on-off" switch, like the machine they thought he was, there would have been no question of shutting him down for the night. However, thanks to fate, no such switch existed—yet.

…twenty-three… twenty-two… twenty-one…

The countdown continued uninterrupted. It never ceased: the benefit of a computerized brain.

The neural-network nano-chip implanted in the association area of his artificial parietal lobe was hard-wired to the sentient, synthetic neuronal arrays floating in a bed of liquid, smart-memory polymers. Operating as a whole, they served as his cerebral cortex. Unlike anything created by nature, his cybernetic brain function was accessible to his conscious mind on demand. This unique feature offered Abe the option of monitoring and tweaking his internal development. At optimum levels, his conscious and subconscious multitasking mind processed complex problems like a computer, only at three orders of magnitude faster and twice the rate of current robotic models. Most of his brain operated in this accelerated state, except for one segment. It functioned at a lower level, allowing him to participate in conversations using his frontal lobe like a human.

A faint quiver slithered through his body from an electrical surge. His mind had penetrated and engaged an online access point on the G-Net.

Abe routinely connected to the internet. His cyberspace vocabulary was extensive, allowing him to read, with ease, the raw data that flowed at him. He conversed in every available form of superset and subset encoding online and whipped through database languages and web protocols without hesitation. But there was a snag; there was always a snag. His was time. Abe had no choice but to limit his duration online for many reasons, but the primary related to his composition. Human physiology hampered his ability to sustain prolonged connections. While a permanent connection was desirable, it was not advisable or even possible. Still, he had a margin of latitude and logged-on at every opportunity.

Accessing, reading, and retrieving all forms of available networked data, raw or otherwise, were not where his talents ended, but where they began. Thanks to another loophole in security protocols, Abe could hack anything that the Global Union and other organizations put online.

As he patched into the GU "Public Monitoring System," his lips curled at an acronym that had earned scorn and snide remarks for decades. From here, Abe could track anyone or anything, and go anywhere the tentacles of the internet went. For now, he focused on MACC staff, and more precisely, his lab team.

Nan rarely arrived at work on time. Today would be no exception. She had reset the snooze button on her Palmcom three times before her apartment registered activity. Abe monitored the online sensor for electrical consumption at her address. It whizzed along as she showered, dried her fiery hair, and brushed her teeth. Abe knew that by the time Nan dressed, applied makeup, programmed the Kleanbot, switched on the alarm system, and entered and exited the Hypertube to stroll through MACC's glass doors, she would be approximately thirteen minutes behind her scheduled arrival time.

Ken and Rajon would also arrive approximately five minutes later than their usual six to eight-minute tardiness. Abe knew this with logical certainty. While tracking Nan, he'd followed their progress as well. Online reports suggested heavy traffic flow and a nine-minute delay due to rain. Surveillance spotted the luxury Tesla sports car running caution lights as Ken overrode auto-drive to shave minutes from their commute, but bad weather and carpooling with Rajon had distracted him. The men were preoccupied and predictable. Traffic cameras displayed exaggerated movements inside the car between the balding, badly sunburned driver and his black-haired passenger. Heavy rain and their heated debate over two archaic graphic novel franchises would slow Ken's response time and their progress by more than two minutes.

Abe dipped his head in an indiscernible nod to himself. Security cameras spotted the electric vehicle wheeling into the parking lot. Abe continued to predict their progress. After plugging in the car, Ken and Rajon would dash up the walkway through the torrential downpour to palm the hand scanner. Rushing through the front doors of the building, they would flash their security cards at the guard and then ride the elevator to lab level. Still engaged in debate, both men would head for the locker room, dry off, wash up, and change into lab garb. Shortly after that, they would arrive at their destination, roughly twelve minutes late.

Abe raised his head and opened his eyes, severing the online link. He sat poised and motionless, his face softening as his human-like thoughts shifted, with a noted degree of eagerness, toward the other missing employee, Tamera Yvette Everett. The silent room made her absence more noticeable. How strange that he missed her presences, even for a short while. But he did. He missed the sound of her voice with its soft, subtle Creole cadence. He missed, even more, the probing gaze of her almond-shaped chestnut eyes, and the pleasing aesthetics of her heart-shaped face framed by long black hair. So often the curly mass poked out from under a surgical cap, refusing to be restrained. The beauty of her wide smile, high cheekbones, and smooth Caribbean features stood in stark contrast to her cut and dried demeanor. The clonedroid project manager and neurogeneticist with a sub-specialization in robotics, Dr. Everett, never ran late. Today, Tamera had arrived earlier than usual, reporting to an emergency meeting. The high-level assembly and press interview to follow would delay her arrival at the lab. Abe lowered his eyes, and his shoulders slumped. Something within him deflated.

His thoughts shifted back to focus on the other team members, all of whom would arrive shortly. Although accomplished specialists in their own right, the lab technicians tended to be as dismissive toward Tamera as they were toward Abe. Regard for company brass held even less significance to them. But today would be different. Abe knew that the hard-hearted orders, soon to be passed down to Tamera, would grab her staff's attention, and be met with varying degrees of resistance.

This will be an interesting day.

2

...twenty-two hours forty-eight minutes eight seconds... seven... six...

Reaching for a large jug from a nearby utility cart that doubled as a nightstand, Abe remained seated on the examination table and waited. He sipped water and listened for the muffled sound of voices, picturing the two men on their way to the lab. The tall, lean Rajon strolled effortlessly as the shorter-legged Ken broke a sweat keeping pace.

Ken remained oblivious to everything around him. His ginger brows knitted into a frown, and he flailed his arms as he walked and argued with Rajon. In contrast, his black-haired coworker greeted other employees with a nod as the two men entered the elevator and descended to lab level.

As the pair moved forward along the corridor, Rajon maintained a near-expressionless demeanor. Until the formation of the GU, Aboriginal Peoples living on North American reservations had, for the most part, lived like outcasts on the very land of their heritage. As a result, many Native Americans of the First Nations, like Rajon, remained guarded. Treaties, borders, and reservations no longer existed, and everyone stood on equal ground—in theory. But old prejudices die hard. Ray Jon Pine, the descendant of an Ojibwa chief, had faced stigma on more than one occasion, and far too many obstacles in perusing his chosen path. With time, his name Ray Jon naturally morphed into Rajon. In his muted, polite manner, he did little to correct false assumptions. Misconceptions about his name and heritage prevailed, along with a stereotype that proved lucrative as he advanced his career in the field of science.

Abe felt a kinship with him, or more, with Rajon's ancestors and the sting of their alienation. Like all governments before it, the Global Union had played a role, making things worse while feigning to make the world a better place. As the self-proclaimed founder of human-race unification, the GU took credit for something not altogether within its right to claim.

Unification had transpired not so much as the result of a political mechanism, but due to the introduction of robotic beings into homes in every corner of the developed world. Abe had long ago realized that nothing unifies divided groups faster than the introduction of a new element. The "us versus them" attitude had shifted. Friction no longer festered to the same degree that it once had between the peoples of the world. Contempt still existed, even to a greater extent than before, but it now flowed less between humans and more in a downward direction, from humanity toward its creation.

Abe lifted his gaze, focusing now on the spoken words he had detected beyond the lab. The words grew louder, but the full conversation remained too faint to identify, even for Abe's sensitive ears. The first set of access doors swished open then closed. The voices grew. Two sets of fast-paced, squeaking steps cleared the second set of doors. Voices rose in decibel, but only words said with emphasis stood out.

"…Wa…bet!"

"…bull...it…"

Swishshlunk

"DAMN STRAIGHT…gainst…caped dude…"

"NO WAY…he'd ram that cigar…so fast…"

"…Can't die…got...dum...tium…He'd crush bat…"

SHLICK…THUNK

"You *think* so."

"No dude, I *know* so."

Another set of doors closed. The two techs garbed in blue scrubs, white sneakers, and surgical caps emerged to stand outside the lab.

They palmed the biometric scanners. Their voices rose and fell in heated conversation as the shorter, red-faced man tapped a security code into the keypad. Both men strode through the opened glass door and into the lab, ignoring protocol and Abe entirely. Rajon and Ken were still arguing as the lab door sealed with a *shwick* behind them.

"He'd kick that candy-ass so fast it'd make your empty head spin," Ken said.

Rajon shook his head. "Never happen, dude. That putz couldn't kick a football. My guy would slice that wimpy caped dude to bits."

"Huh, in your graphic dreams, maybe," Ken huffed as he moved toward the coffee pot.

"Oh, my God. You guys still on that crap?" A petite, freckled woman entered the lab and jabbed Rajon playfully in the ribs with a raven-black fingernail.

He jumped and squeaked, then spun around. "DAMMIT Nan. Stop doin' that."

A snotty grin graced her maroon lips as arctic eyes flashed a wink. Spikes of cherry hair poked out from beneath her cap as she shook her head and continued, "Get over it. I don't need to hear that crap again today. I could care less which cartoon character has more testosterone."

"*Superhero,*" both men retorted in unison.

"Like it matters." She dismissed them with a wave of her hand. "Seriously, you two need to get a grip on life and get a girlfriend, or at least, get laid. Well, in your case," she finger-pistoled Ken, "get a blow-up doll."

"Like you're the expert," Ken retorted, snatching a

MACC mug from the tray next to the coffee machine.

"I'll put points on it that I have more fun than you do," Nan smiled as she picked up an empty metal tray from a rolling stand, then made her way to a supply cabinet and began to rummage through it. "You know, the term 'married to the business' isn't meant to be taken literally."

"Ready, set, *aaand*…" Rajon mimicked a sportscaster as he drained coffee into a mug that stated in red block letters, *SCREW LAB SAFETY - THIS TECH WANTS SUPERPOWERS*. Ken held out his dull company mug, and Rajon filled it, too. Ken ignored the courtesy and moved toward his chair, still focused on Nan.

"So, tell me cyber-*chica*, exactly how lucky did *you* get last night?"

Nan arched a well-contoured eyebrow and stabbed Ken with her gaze.

"…*They're off*," Rajon announced, leaning against the counter to sip coffee. His dark eyes flipped between the other two.

"Let me guess." Ken slid into the chair next to his station. "You had a steamy moment with a dragon while playing Dungeons and Dumbasses, or did you get a good deal on batteries?" he chuckled. Ken's overly-bleached teeth stood in contrast against his lobster-colored skin. "Am I getting warm?"

Nan's eyes narrowed. "Nah, you're as cold as ever, Ken. But it's not like anyone would call you hot."

Clonedroid: The New Wave

Rajon sputtered, snorting coffee through his nose. "Shit!" He snatched a paper towel from the dispenser and proceeded to wipe coffee from his hands and lab coat. "You two bicker like an old married couple."

Silence chilled the room. Ken and Nan glared at Rajon. He waved the paper towel like a white flag. "Sorry."

Flashing one last warning look at him, Nan turned back to the overindulged, over-groomed man across from her as she placed supplies on the metal tray. "Ken, lemme speak in a language that your limited mind can process." She raised her free hand and offered a one finger salute.

"The level of professionalism in this place never fails to amuse," Rajon snickered and sauntered toward his seat.

Ignoring him, Ken remained locked on Nan. "That's the kind of uneducated response I'd expect from a non-Ivy League, Midwest bumpkin...."

Abe observed the three in silence. To those around him, he had blended into the backdrop, and today, he preferred it that way.

To a casual observer, Abe may have appeared to be impassive, even disassociated. On the contrary, he remained attentive to the endless stream of data that presented itself to him. His mind could, and had, engaged in hundreds of tasks at once. Even though most segments of his brain were preoccupied with technical and abstract processes, Abe never missed a hue of change in the external world around him. He monitored everything within his reach, recorded it, and filed it away. Watching and listening now, as he had every day before this, he observed how MACC staff interacted, individually and as a structured whole. He examined how they responded to stimuli daily within their confined surroundings.

The evaluation of human behavior was crucial. Abe had been granted authorization to study whatever resources MACC had to offer and that, in turn, had allowed humans to monitor his progress. Thus, he had taken advantage of all opportunities as they presented themselves and absorbed all available data in many diverse disciplines, but most extensively in science. More specifically, he had targeted Homo sapiens in his quest to examine the interaction of living things over time within their environment. His study of humans, those who studied him, remained a primary objective and an integral part of his purpose. Still, Abe never lost track of the countdown or his goal today as he sat, expressionless and unmoving, observing the people before him.

"You're an ass-hat, Ken." Nan frowned as she closed the cabinet door and set the fully stocked tray on the countertop.

"And that attitude has gotten you nowhere, Miss Nancy Anne Lee." Ken's voice dripped with condescension. "Maybe, someday you'll get promoted, but it'll be long after I've moved up and moved on."

"Preferably, moved on," she said.

"You're not even published," he said, dismissing her comment. "And you expect management to take notice? I've been here less time than either of you and have more clout than you two combined. I'm rising to the top."

Shaking her head, Nan snickered. "Yeah, that's cause shit floats."

Rajon chuckled and slid into his chair to watch the show unfold. He yawned, then sipped more coffee, waiting for the caffeine to work its magic.

…twenty-two hours eleven minutes fifty-three seconds… fifty-two… fifty-one…

Precious seconds ticked away while Abe continued to observe the trivial banter in stoic silence. The derisive disposition of the staff today did nothing to change anything vital in the larger scope of those things long since set in motion. It only meant that this performance might continue until Tamera appeared and ended the backbiting, or until Nan tired of the routine.

But something in the atmosphere and their body language had shifted. Abe knew, with relative ease and absolute certainty, that only seconds remained before Nan's short attention span kicked in to shut this sideshow down.

"Not that this hasn't been *really* boring, Ken, but

we've all got work to do before the wicked witch of the West Nile virus arrives. And I'm fine without another lecture on team participation," Nan said, pulling surgical gloves from a sealed container.

Rajon nodded and swiveled around to face his desk. Leaning forward, he uncoupled the Palmcom from his wristband, mated it to the wafer-thin DeskPad unit that covered his workstation, and tapped its black surface. A virtual keyboard flickered into existence on the pad, and a double-monitor popped up to float before his eyes. "Speakin' of the devil, where is she?" Rajon asked. He scanned the virtual clock on the screen as he leaned back again.

Ken raised his mug to his lips, sniffed then froze. His hazel eyes shifted from the flickering screen to the frothing liquid in his cup. "How do you people drink this sludge?" His brow wrinkled. "This is why I hate carpooling. I'd have made it to Java Joint and been on time if not for you." He flashed an angry look at Rajon.

"*Me?*" Rajon said.

Ken dismissed him and looked back at the screen. Rajon's earlier question sank in, and Ken answered as much to himself as to his colleagues. "Correct me if I'm wrong, but the *scheduler* lists Tamera attending a high-level meeting this morning?" He tapped his keyboard and squinted at the screen, then looked back at the other two. "Either of you know anything about that?"

"Not a thing. You?" Rajon tilted his head and looked

questioningly at Nan.

Nan shrugged as she snapped a surgical glove into place. "Don't know. Don't care," she replied, then picked up the stocked tray and moved towards Abe, addressing him rhetorically. "So, how's 2112 today…?"

3

Dr. Tamera Everett shifted with impatience in the conference room leather chair. So far, this meeting felt no different than any other dull business discussion she had fidgeted through in the past. Somehow, this high-level gathering was supposed to be different, not the same old corporate off-gassing. Last night's emergency board of directors meeting, something she had never attended, had prompted this early-hour executive committee meeting, also something she had never attended, until now. All of MACC's senior-ranking staff had crammed into the room. Tamera felt awkward sitting shoulder to shoulder with so many executives who had no idea who she was or how extensively she contributed to their pocket change.

Perched on the edge of her seat, she had waited for a crisis to unfold. Instead, the nasal-voiced CFO had addressed the group. Nearly an hour had passed, and Brad continued to ramble on about the need for budget restrictions. It was his usual spiel about squeezing more out of less and expecting everything in return. Tamera had no idea what made his drivel so urgent. She had heard all of this before. Management could squeeze all they liked, but investor interest rode on her designs. It rode on Abe, the ultimate product. Cutbacks listed on company letterhead had no impact on her project.

Tamera's eyes panned around the posh conference room filled with glass furniture and lifeless black and white prints. The balmy temperature and recessed lighting did nothing to add warmth. Even though this room lacked the bright sterility that dominated the rest of the building, its extravagant décor provided little appeal. It possessed far less humanity than her lab. Only the fingerprints smeared across a slick tabletop provided a human touch. Tamera cringed and sank further into her chair. Sucking in a deep breath and blinking several times to stay awake, she refocused on the man seated beside her, Dr. Samuel E. Miller. Sam was her boss, and he held a high-level position as the Chief Medical Director and Executive Committee Member. A frown had filled his face as he sat with arms crossed over his chest, eyes forward, staring at nothing and no one in particular. Sam intimidated a lot of people at MACC. He was blunt and demanding, but Tamera appreciated his no-nonsense style. Her eyes skimmed over several other executives and attendees then focused on the person seated commandingly at the head of the table. Stiff, expressionless, and in a dominant pose, sat the president and co-founder of MACC, Lorraine Gantrua.

A geneticist and a shrewd businesswoman, Lorraine along with her robotics engineer husband, Neville, had transformed a small disadvantaged robotics shop into a sci-fi nerd's wet dream. Within ten years, they had merged two scientific passions: cloning and robotics. Within ten more, they had expanded into Living Artificial Intelligence and pioneered production of the world's first functional humanoid androids. With federal funding, shareholder backing, and Lorraine's cutthroat skills, MACC emerged as a leader in the industry. After Neville's unexpected death, she assumed majority control, and with additional GU support, forged the company into a global giant.

Now, the president sat rigid, chin high, and hands folded on the tabletop. With blue eyes as cold as a mountain stream, Lorraine scanned the room. Her elongated face and long nose were framed by straight, white hair cut to a bob in the same sharp angle as her jawline. Its severity matched her personality. As far as Tamera was concerned, Lorraine was better-suited to riding a broom than a corporate jet. She also believed that the president's depth of character possessed the same superficial warmth as her thin, over-polished smile. It was a strained expression that only surfaced during Lorraine's rare attempts to convey friendliness, but employees knew better. The president of MACC tolerated little verbal repartee with staff and utilized intimidation well. It kept employees submissive, but Tamera had no love for corporate politics or bureaucratic bullshit. As a result, tensions between the two had grown heated at times. If Dr. Tamera Everett's work in the lab had been any less vital to the corporate bottom line, Lorraine would have tossed her to the curb long ago. Out of concern for the corporation's best interests, Sam limited contact between the two women—a wise move, and one that worked best for Tamera.

Lorraine stood up, flashed a mock smile, and motioned the Chief Financial Officer to take his seat. "Thank you, Brad, I think we get the picture." She shot a steel-clad glance down one side of the table and up the other. "You may be wondering why we convened an emergency meeting this morning. Well, for those not in the know, I will make you privy to some sensitive information." Lorraine paused. Her words settled over the room like radioactive fallout. Significant glances shot from subordinates to directors who ignored the imploring looks. All eyes shifted back to the president. "The company is facing a series of in-depth GU investigations."

Gasps erupted, and Lorraine held up a hand to silence the group. Groans died away, and a hush fell over the room. She now had everyone's full attention, including Tamera's.

"I'm sure you've all seen headlines attempting to tarnish our image and wondered why. Apparently, we were wrong when we thought we'd won over public support for our new line. We now face financial scrutiny and a media roasting of our cybernetic and human parts, thanks to ludicrous claims by an anonymous whistleblower. Confidential information is being bled to the press, along with a steady stream of misinformation, stirring up an old shit storm."

"God, here we go again," someone from the other side of the table lamented. Heads bobbed, and sighs of remembrance followed.

"Not if I can help it," Lorraine snapped. "Yes, there's a revival of anti-clone sentiment, activists picketing again, and of course, the media is looking to cash in on it. And yes, we'll need to open our books and coffers to GU Regulators to prove ourselves, *yet again*." Lorraine held up a hand to subdue furrowed brows. "But, we'll be fine," she said. "It's a smear campaign by a competitor to stall the clonedroid go-live date. As always, we'll prevail. We've come through tougher times to get this far," Lorraine sighed. "That said, I want staff on their best behavior. I want auditors to receive complete cooperation from all employees and all departments. Is that understood!"

Heads bobbed in unison, but confusion lingered on faces. Nervous glances flashed like lightning up and down the table.

"Keep this confidential. MACC will legally pursue anyone who speaks out of turn."

Again, heads nodded.

"Audits will commence in a few days and proceed for several weeks, forcing us to push back the production start date."

Heads turned, and murmurs grew. Matt, the Chief Operations Officer, interrupted. "Just how far back are we talking?"

"Possibly a few months," Lorraine said with a voice as grim as the expression on her face.

Protests filled the room.

"We can't delay that long," Matt said.

The Director of Sales and Marketing jumped in. "I agree. The new line is nearly ready for harvesting and orders are stacking high. Hospitals around the world need transplant organs. This is *exactly* what we can't afford right now. This could kill us, and our customers, literally—"

Matt cut back in. "What about workloads and overtime? My department is pushing maximums. We can't afford to stop now and play nanny to a bunch of bean counters, then be expected to burn additional candlelight to meet deadlines. We shouldn't have to justify ourselves to more pencil-pushing bureaucrats because of some damn hoax—"

BAM

Tamera and half the room jumped as Lorraine

slammed her well-decorated, manicured hand on the tabletop.

"I'm aware of that." Lorraine's voice boomed across the room. "Yes, there will be increased workloads. Yes, we must play nice with the GU again. And, yes, I understand employees are working overtime, but this is temporary. And let me remind you, a part of doing business. Audits will impact cost centers, but we have contingencies. I have no doubt we'll recoup outlay before the end of fourth-quarter. So, let's keep our heads on and move forward. I've drafted an action plan for all departments that I'll forward shortly. We'll meet again tomorrow, and I'll consider your suggestions at that time. Until then, keep this info under your hat. The media already has enough of our parts to gnaw at without tossing them more scraps."

With that, Lorraine stepped away from the table and moved toward the door without a second glance at anyone. Tamera watched the stern woman in the canary designer suit march through the door and wondered if Lorraine also owned a coat fashioned from a large litter of Dalmatian pups.

4

As the meeting drew to an end, members stood and padded out of the room behind Lorraine, saving their discontent until they were beyond earshot of the president. Tamera fingered the Palmcom on her wristband to check the time, then grabbed her empty green tea jar from the table and prepared to file out behind the rest.

Someone tapped her on the shoulder. "Tamera, wait. I need to speak with you," Sam said.

Turning to face her boss, she nodded. Together they stood off to one side and waited for the room to empty.

As a former GU Medical Commissioner, Sam had a firm grasp on the business, bureaucratic, and medical affairs of MACC. Possibly past his prime, he still looked lean, mean, and proud of remaining that way, something Tamera had respected. But today, she found no reassurance in the green eyes that squinted at her, or in the frown that had hardened Sam's face.

When the sound of shuffling feet had died away,

Sam addressed her, sounding more serious than usual. "As you've no doubt gathered, the company is facing a rocky road."

Tamera nodded. A frown formed on her face that deepened to match his.

"There's a lot more to this than Lorraine lets on," he continued. "We'll be under the invasive microscope far longer than our president wants to admit. We're facing some heavy investigations, coming at us from all divisions: taxation, technology, environment, along with the securities and global exchange commission, and that's just for starters."

Tamera's nose wrinkled. "What?"

"And trust me. Audits are the least of our worries." Sam's grim look intensified, and his voice dipped lower. "Oh, and our Ethics Review Committee is facing an inquiry by the Division of Medicine and Agriculture for human rights violations, all thanks to a specific line of humanoid robots."

Tamera's eyes shot wide. "That's insane."

He nodded. "That's one turd on a growing shit pile. This whole thing couldn't happen at a worse time for us. Lorraine's right. It reeks like an orchestrated plan to steal our competitive advantage."

Eyeing Sam, Tamera realized how tired he looked. He had been unusually tense for weeks, and now she understood why. She motioned to speak, but he raised a hand to mute her.

"Wait. It gets better. And this goes no further than here and now."

Tamera dipped her head in compliance, and the fingers of her right hand tightened around the empty tea bottle.

"We're also under investigation for theft and tax fraud," Sam said. Tamera gasped as he continued. "And Lorraine is being accused of falsifying corporate books and documents to gain GU startup grants."

"Are you serious?"

"Damn straight," he replied.

Tamera had to catch her breath. This level of investigation, regardless of whether accusations were true or false, could end MACC. It could end her project, her team's work, even their careers, all of it, gone.

Her frown deepened. "Do you have any idea who's responsible or where this is coming from?" A multitude of questions sprang to mind, and then regret followed curiosity. Tamera had that uneasy feeling she would dislike the answers or where their discussion was leading.

"No idea," Sam said. "But we're under attack for security exchange violations, as well."

Tamera shook her head. It was absurd. She couldn't believe what she was hearing.

"Something to do with hacking systems and leaking info to manipulate robo-trades to gain an unfair advantage in the market. Just as ludicrous is the communications investigation for using too many G-Net access points without adequate licensing." Sam let a sigh of exasperation filter through clenched teeth. "Of course, no one internally claims knowledge that any of this happened. Our Information Technology Department assures us we have licenses for all access points, but the V-NANS indicates otherwise. It's as if someone has hacked our system, but if so, they've left no footprint."

"How is that possible?"

Sam shrugged. "The Commission claims a great deal of pirating occurred for years. IT failed to identify it and now screams ignorance. We're going to incur enormous fines. Somehow, we need to keep the press upwind of the stink." Sam raised a brow toward her.

"Understood," Tamera said. The fingers on her left hand fidgeted with the seam inside her lab coat pocket while her other hand white-knuckled the bottle she still held.

"To make it worse," Sam said with a sigh, "Most of our executives and board members are facing personal investigations. Accusations are trumped-up, but that's no consolation prize."

"Unbelievable." She hesitated and then braved it. "Including you?"

"So far, no," Sam's shoulders fell a little. "But my good fortune is a two-sided blade."

Dark brows met above her eyes. She wrinkled her

nose in a silent question.

Sam frowned at Tamera's confusion. "Right now, I'm the only one standing in the clear. "So, guess where that leaves me…?"

"*Oh.*"

Sam scowled. "That's right, looks like I'm a traitor—or someone in my employ. And I won't stand for false accusations or treachery," he continued. "I intend to make damn certain my department emerges as the saving grace of this company. So, that brings me to you."

"Me?"

Sam nodded. "I need you to be my eyes and ears," he said. "It's obvious we have an internal leak, and they have a real hate for MACC." Anger danced in his eyes, and his tone held an edge that made her take a step back. "We've carved out a solid code of ethics and justified our intentions to agencies and advocates once already. And damn it, I hate covering the same ground twice. But as Lorraine said, it's business as usual. Let the officials and lawyers hammer out deals. You and I need to win this battle at ground level. I'll handle logistics for our department. And you…" He leveled a stern look upon Tamera. "I've scheduled you for an important interview."

Tamera gawked at Sam.

"I was scheduled to meet with a reporter this morning, but now, I think it would be better if you met with him instead." Sam raised his wrist and looked down at his Palmcom. "In about five minutes," he added.

"What?" Heat flooded her face.

"He's a blogger with the online media. Shawn… something." Sam looked back at her, his jaw set and firm. "He's a tech nerd dying to do a report on our new line. The guy's got a huge following and solid fan base. We need him on our side. And what I need is for you to make him giddy about what we do. Give him a positive spin."

"Sam—"

"—And I need you to be the face of MACC," he continued. "Explain that we're making the world a better place. Your sweet smile in a photo along with some good press can only help us. You know the product line better than anyone. As its designer, this is a no-brainer for you. You can defend our company in the media with a genuine, heart-warming story. Turn on the charm. Be engaging. Be personable. Sell the clonedroid line, and sell it well. Your story will save lives, Tamera. It can save MACC."

Tamera's stomach tightened as Sam attempted but failed to generate a sincere smile. She shook her head. "You know I'm not good at this sort of thing. I'm not prepared. What am I supposed to say? What do I, I—"

"Relax. Be yourself. It's no different than the lecture you gave at the university or an interview for a peer review journal. I've seen you in action. You can handle this."

Tamera scrunched her face. "Sam, I don't think this is a good—"

"—Apart from running interference for the company, I also need you to get the team geared up. I'm counting on my crew to come through for us."

The warm room was suffocating her. "I don't understand. What more can we do?" she asked.

"I'm getting to that." Annoyance crept into his voice. His fake smile had disappeared. "Since we're pushing back production deadlines, there's only one way to move forward. We need something tangible to dispel rumors. Our lobbyists are working hard to influence officials, but sadly, it's a process that takes too long and just not enough time exists. So, we need to offer the world successful organ transplants, and it's imperative that we do it now. It'll be a small token of good faith. It'll assure everyone that all is well at MACC." Sam shifted his weight and clasped his hands behind his back. "Along with your interview, a couple of successful transplants will give the world a good taste of what we offer. It'll snap attitudes around in a hurry. It'll tell the public that delays will be detrimental to them and their loved ones. It'll also demonstrate to bureaucrats that we're providing a public good and put pressure on them to leave us alone. Not to mention, it'll send a damn clear message to our competitors that we're unbreakable. Transplants will generate support and buy us time to get back on track. It'll also weed out the traitor. Then we'll crucify that fucker."

"I understand MACC's needs, but I still don't follow you," Tamera said. "Our new line hasn't passed final quality inspection yet. If we put it on hold, where are we going to get the donor organs needed to meet this good faith order?"

"Isn't that obvious?" Sam said. "We only have one fully operational Clonedroid."

"Abe? You want to sacrifice our prototype?"

"Yes. Is there a problem with that?" Sam raised a bushy brow.

"*Hell—Yes!*" Tamera snapped. Rage flushed her face.

Sam's eyes bulged. For the first time, Tamera had set him back on his heels. She even caught herself by surprise. She'd never been fully insubordinate before, but his request provoked deep-seated anger she had no idea existed. It emerged from nowhere but felt instinctive. She had to defend her work, defend Abe.

Tilting his head backward, Sam barked out a laugh. His eyes came back to meet hers. As his chuckles trickled away, her anger intensified, and the heat in her cheeks spread to the tips of her ears.

"You *are* amusing," he chuckled.

"I'm serious. You're not chopping up Abe for organ transplants."

Sam's face hardened again. "Stop referring to 2112 as

Clonedroid: The New Wave

Abe. If you humanize it, you make this harder than it needs to be. I understand your reservations. I know you pioneered the project, but we don't have the luxury of holding onto it. We have viable models readying for production, so we don't need 2112 anymore. But we need the positive results those organs will provide."

"How can you say that? He's a fully conscious model. We have an incredible opportunity to study him—or in business terms—study a valuable asset that can benefit us." She flapped her arms. It took all her strength not to hurl the empty jar at him. "Sam, we'd be discarding years of painstaking research and a chance to learn more about what we've created. We still know so little about him and the effects of his engineering on the human body. *Seriously?* What are you thinking?"

Tamera tried to huff away the tension, but her body only grew more rigid. Her anger didn't faze Sam as he spoke in a low tone of polite patronization.

"Look, I understand you see this as a setback—"

"*Setback!?*"

"—But," he said as he raised an index finger, "this is an opportunity. We can't afford to put time and resources into 2112 when that model can save lives and boost our image. It's the only model ready with harvestable goods, and we need them. End of story." Sam said. "Don't go soft, Tamera. You know what's at stake. The time for study has passed." He inclined his head toward her. "Scientists are no different than butchers. You know better than to get attached to the livestock."

Tamera gawked at him then she shook her head in frustration. "We're talking about *Abe*, not some poor, ear-marked cow."

"See, that's what I mean—"

"—*Damn it*, Sam. Abe's not a side of beef to be carved up and shipped out to keep shareholders happy. He's a conscious, advanced model for a reason—so, we can learn from him. He can teach us so much more about ourselves, about DNA, RNA, robotics, humanoid design, and biomechanics, not to mention cloning. The potential to learn from Abe is endless. We need to study him. How can we head off unforeseen issues with lab-grown organs if we're not aware of how his cells react over time? We need Abe alive to stay one step ahead. That's his purpose."

"Not this time, not with this one," Sam growled. His thick brows knitted together.

Tamera's voice rose in exasperation, "Any gain we make now from his organs will not outweigh our loss down the road. *Please*, don't do this. Think of long-term consequences."

"Long-term is meaningless if we don't survive the short-term. You need to think beyond the lab for once."

"I am," Tamera replied.

"*No*. You're letting emotion cloud professional judgment. It's bad enough you named the damn thing, but now you're hindering progress. I've given you plenty of leeway, but this has gone on long enough—"

"You're damn right it has, "she snapped. "It's gone on *too* long."

Sam cocked an eyebrow. "Finish the interview. Then return to the lab and prepare prototype 2112 for delivery to the processing plant. Unless…" he said, glaring at her, "you're unable to finish the job we hired you to do. If so, perhaps you'd like the rest of the day off to reevaluate your position while someone else does your job for you."

Tamera stared at Sam. It felt like he had slapped her across the face.

"Is that a threat?" she asked. Blood raced through her body and rang in her ears. He had tolerated a lot of her insubordinate remarks in the past, usually giving in and rallying behind her if she presented a reasonable argument. But this had blindsided her. Sam was the last person who would stoop to issuing threats to press a point.

"Take it however you like. If you're unfit, we'll find someone else. But there's no further discussion on the matter. Are we clear?"

She drew in a breath and braced herself. Blood still hammered past her eardrums. Then slowly, reluctantly, she swallowed her pride and nodded, "I'll do it." She lowered her head and voice in defeat.

"Good," he sighed, and she detected relief. Tamera

looked back at him and found it hard to stifle her anger. A thin smile inched over Sam's face as he reached out and patted her on the shoulder. "I don't blame you for wanting to protect the prototype, but we need to protect the company's interests first. If not, we jeopardize more than 2112. There's no room for error or personal feelings to get in the way."

Tamera nodded.

"So, we're on the same page?"

"Yes," she sighed, "but it'll take time to get 2112 prepped. *And*, I don't want anyone breathing down my neck."

"Fine," Sam said flatly, all business again. "You've got until close today to prep him." Pivoting on his heel, Sam marched out of the room.

Tamera shook her head and stood in silence. Too many concerns flashed through her mind all at once: *What the hell just happened? How can Sam agree to this? What will I say to the others? How will we do this, at all, let alone on time? This feels all wrong. God, why did I let Sam pressure me like that? How can I possibly go through with this?*

Beads of perspiration broke across her forehead as thoughts crowded her mind. Then one thought in particular drowned out everything else and provoked a cold sweat.

Oh, SHIT. What do I tell Abe?

Her stomach lurched. She closed her eyes and took a

Clonedroid: The New Wave

deep breath of stale air to regain composure.

"Lights out," Tamera said through gritted teeth.

The conference room shut down.

5

So, how's 2112 today?

Nan's lackluster greeting lingered as she moved forward.

Seated on the examining table, jug of water in hand, Abe dipped his head in polite acknowledgment as she approached with the instrument tray. "I am well. How are you?" he asked.

Nan flashed a thin-lipped smile that offered the same degree of tepid-warmth that he had displayed in his greeting toward her.

"Peachy," she replied.

The perfume of heavily-fragranced soap and Jasmine shampoo reached him before she did. It tickled his nose, but he refused to flinch.

The tray of instruments jangled as she plopped it onto the wheeled cart that stood to the left of Abe. "No real complaints. Well, maybe one." She cast a snide look over her shoulder toward Ken, then brought her eyes back to the cart and started sorting through items on the tray. "Your breakfast will arrive soon, so let's get these tests out of the way. Then you can dig in when it gets here." Glancing up at Abe, she said, "You must be starving?"

Abe nodded. He was.

Apart from the colorless conversation between Nan and her subject, the room had fallen silent. Ken and Rajon ignored them. They also ignored each other and settled into sipping coffee and tapping away at the shimmering keys at their workstations.

Grabbing a disinfectant packet from the tray, Nan turned toward her subject. Abe knew the daily procedure. Without speaking, he disrobed his top-half, sliding the blue V-necked tunic over his head. Folding it with precision, he placed it neatly to his right on the examination table.

Nan looked at his shirt, then at the table, then back at him, and shook her head. "I don't get why you won't use the cot. The cot is comfortable. That is not." She nodded at the metal table with her freckled nose.

The comment was more rumination to herself than a question to Abe, but her repetitive reaction amused him. It fascinated him how humans could ask the same question, repeatedly, knowing the answer would remain unchanged.

The strong bitter scent of the antiseptic swab stung Abe's nose. Why he had not grown accustomed to its intensity remained a mystery, but like everything else in the lab, he had learned to ignore it or live with it. Instinctively, he tightened his hand into a fist and pumped it several times then extended his arm out toward Nan. She lightly slapped a vein on the back of his hand to raise it in preparation for the needle.

Abe sat unmoving and silent as Nan sterilized the spot on his hand. He watched as she swapped the pungent alcohol swab for a small black device from the tray. Now she focused on extracting a sample of his blood: "You know the drill. This may sting a bit."

Closing his eyes lightly, Abe twitched as she pricked his vein with the now extended retractable needle. His reaction to this procedure and all medical tests provoked the same human response: confusion. Without looking, he knew that Nan frowned at him as she removed the device, applied pressure to the pinhole in his hand, and set the device back on the tray. The practice of drawing blood was quick and relatively painless when compared with the obsolete process from a few decades earlier that required needles and vials. Even children no longer flinched at having blood drawn. No doubt, Nan and the rest of the team wondered why a mechanically-minded clonedroid winced at the test every time. Truthfully, his reaction was not a physical response to the mining of his blood, but the transmission of related data.

Abe opened his eyes.

Nan dabbed the back of his hand with a cotton swab.

The tiny trickle of blood had stopped. "Good. Now for the rest of our chamber of horrors routine," she said, grabbing more alcohol swabs from the tray and preparing to attach electrodes to his body.

Abe glanced down at the tray, eyeing the black device she had placed there moments earlier. The needle sat fully retracted now. A small light flashed green, indicating that the instrument had completed an analysis of his blood, transmitted the results to the network, and sterilized the needle. A hint of a smile curved Abe's lips as he stared at the gadget.

Interception successful. Transmission complete.

With a great deal of work still to do, he maintained his current link to V-NANS and the G-Net, the connection established seconds before blood extraction and device transmission.

...twenty-one hours fifty-five minutes fifty seconds... forty-nine... forty-eight...

"Please, let me help," Abe said. He picked up three wireless electrodes from the tray at his side.

Nan nodded and passed him a few more. With the remainder in her hands, she stepped around behind him. Abe placed the sucker electrodes in the correct spots on his chest and abdomen. Nan suction-cupped several more to his upper and lower back and arms.

Abe continued to engage Nan in courteous conversation while he maintained the countdown and focused on several additional critical tasks, such as altering existing files. After interrupting the flow of data between the phlebotomy device and the network, he had changed the values of the blood tests and retransmitted them to the system. Momentarily, those altered results would be retrieved and reviewed by Rajon. Abe now intended to do the same with the electrodes, once they began transmitting. This process remained a daily routine, one implemented almost from the moment Tamera had breathed life into him. The real values of his medical information were filed internally, within his nano-chip. There, the truth remained locked and inaccessible to anyone other than himself.

All records and personal identifiers for model 2112 housed within MACC, including blood-type and DNA, had been modified. For years, Abe had provided MACC staff with the results they had expected and not the truth that existed. MACC medical files did not reflect the higher-than-normal levels of enzymes and biochemical indicators of true clonedroid body and brain function, or the higher-than-expected processing speed of his nano-chip. The reality of Abe's stats would have tipped scales and raised flags. If humans knew his potential, his existence would have differed markedly from the current situation, impeding his mobility and access to resources. So, today's results for model 2112 remained consistent with those archived at MACC on prior days, weeks, months, and years.

Clonedroid: The New Wave

CBC - Full Blood Count for Specimen/Model: 2112				
Code	Description	Value	Range	Flags
MACCS-WCC	White cell count	5.62	4.0-10.5	-
MACCS-RCC	Red cell count	5.8	4.5-6.0	-
MACCS-HGB	Hemoglobin	14.8	13.5-17.5	-
MACCS-HCT	Hematocrit	0.439	0.40-0.50	-
MACCS-MCV	Mean corpuscular volume	89.5	80-99	-
MACCS-MCH	Mean corpuscular hemoglobin	30.9	27.0-33.0	-
MACCS-MCHC	MCH concentration	33.1	30.0-34.0	-
MACCS-RDW	Red cell distribution width	13.7	11.5-15.0	-
MACCS-PLT	Platelet count	290	150-450	-
MACCS-MPV	Mean platelet volume	9.9	7.5-11.5	-
MACCS-NE	Neutrophils	3.76	1.5-8.0	-
MACCS-LY	Lymphocytes	1.37	1.0-4.5	-
MACCS-MO	Monocytes	2.88	0.2-0.8	-
MACCS-EO	Eosinophils	0.09	0.0-0.4	-
MACCS-BA	Basophils	0.05	0.0-0.1	-
All levels within normal ranges for adult male specimen age 25-45. No flags noted.				

While Abe chatted with Nan, he continued the countdown and his interruption of the data stream—altering ongoing tests and retransmitting the adjusted values. At the same time, he accessed MACC's security camera feed. On the entrance level, he observed a well-dressed young man sitting in the waiting area of the main lobby. From various angles, Abe watched the man leaf through his undocked Palmcom, impatiently scanning for something. The man hesitated then shook his head and dumped the Palmcom into his sports jacket pocket. He then reached forward and tapped the mini-DeskPad on the arm of his chair. A virtual page shimmered to life, offering a magazine menu. The man keyed in a request. After scanning his face, the screen filled with text from the latest issue of *Scientific Man*, along with a stream of personally-tailored smart-ads.

Peeking through all operational lenses, Abe scrutinized the lab where he sat and spied on other sectors in the lower levels of the building. He tapped into the main production plant, observing a range of products in various stages of creation. Meanwhile, his attention towards MACC's headquarters shifted upwards, and Abe now scanned the corporate offices upstairs. One sparse room on the fifth floor was of particular interest. Beside the door a gold nameplate with bold, black letters advertised *Dr. D. N. Abrams* as the occupant of the office, but no one was inside. The room sat dark and empty.

The day was still early, and conference rooms also remained unoccupied—all but one. The main floor conference room had been active for some time, filled with high-ranking staff. Abe had monitored this meeting off and on since it had begun at seven in the morning and had a good idea what was being said. He could read both body language and lip movements with a ninety-six percent accuracy rate. As he watched, a tall, lean figure with blunt white hair dressed in yellow stood up and assumed control of the meeting. The company's president addressed a large, packed table of individuals. Abe turned his attention to Tamera at the far end. During his prior observations, she had fidgeted with her tea bottle several times and had tapped her Palmcom at predictable intervals, apparently bored with the meeting. Now that had changed. Tamera was leaning forward, her face tense. Astonishment filled her eyes. She would soon learn the secret he already knew.

Continuing his conversation with Nan, Abe fixed and filed the results of his physical examination, maintained the countdown, and watched the corporate security feed. He also accessed several online connections to monitor global activity, gliding through the shocker headlines that filled linked-in monitors around the world.

ETHICAL ISSUES PLAGUE NEWEST MACC MODEL… INVESTIGATIONS BEGIN FOR ANDROID MANUFACTURER… GLOBAL GIANT FIGHTS TO STAY AHEAD IN INDUSTRY… NEW PRODUCT PRODUCES HEADACHES NOT ORGANS… LIVES ARE ON THE PRODUCTION LINE… UNAUTHORIZED G-NET TAPPING ACCUSATIONS… MORE SCANDALS MORE INQUIRIES…

The captions flashed by as Abe scrolled through multiple articles at high speed. It took time to weed through the abundance of sensationalized and inaccurate waffle to find accurate reporting, but he let the data flow.

Abe also watched GU Market stock prices flicker. The series of white on blue numbers that dominated the trading floors changed rapidly with the unstable market. Most stocks had dipped again this morning, resulting from robo-trade instability. The computerized mechanisms installed to safeguard the market had, by their flawed design, destabilized the market further, something the GU wanted to avoid after the financial catastrophe of 2037. The fledgling government struggled to stave off the dark shadow that edged modernized nations ever closer to another global depression. Confidence in the market had waned in recent years, but faith in the government had slid even further. Abe pondered a common human phrase, one hypothesizing that the more something appears to have changed, the more likely it is to have remained unaltered.

It had begun with one whistleblower igniting a lengthy fuse to a much larger and more explosive problem. Then a handful of journalists had started poking around. Stories about the connection between governmental and corporate corruption mounted daily, following on the footfalls of MACC's scandal. Rumor or not, none of it helped an already deteriorating global situation.

Still, the populace remained complacent, optimistic that their system would not fail them entirely. Abe lived by no false ideologies and held to no such illusions. Like all things in the cosmos, even socio-political systems exist within finite environments and decay with time, and faster without adequate maintenance. With this in mind and all probabilities accounted for, the random patterns of a chaotic universe fall into place, and the future becomes predictable. Abe knew, with a high degree of certainty, of only one outcome.

As seconds ticked by, he continued with his tasks, monitoring and interacting with many things at once.

"A hardcover book," Abe responded to Nan's query about the thick black item sitting beside her tray of instruments on the utility cart. "I asked Rajon to bid on it for me."

"Wasting more of our budget for nothing," Ken muttered under his breath.

"What are you, an accountant? Will you just accept it's a part of his training allowance," Rajon muttered back.

Ken sneered. Neither one's eyes lifted from the hypnotic computer screens. "It's still a waste of money," Ken snorted. Rajon shook his head but let the conversation drop.

Abe smiled to himself, remaining focused on his tasks and Nan's questioning look.

"I *know* it's a book. But what is it?" she asked again. "What book is it?"

"The Writings of Thomas Jefferson," he replied.

"But why?" she frowned. "Why would you buy it?"

"To read it." Abe was puzzled.

"No, I mean, why that book?" Nan huffed. "Why not read something more interesting? I bet it's the driest book in the world. Look how thick it is." Her nose wrinkled as she looked from Abe to the book and back again. "Why not something like *Galactic Misfits* by Duffy? Now, that's a fun read. You'd like it. It's an interesting take on terraforming Mars."

"Yes, I've read it," Abe hesitated, then smiled politely. "I agree that it offers an interesting perspective, but I enjoy historical data as well as contemporary."

"So, why not read it online?"

He nodded. "That would be faster," he said. "However, some things, like that rare book," he said, motioning toward the one on the tray, "I prefer in the original physical state. I like to hold them in my hands."

"Hmmm...." Her brow knitted, and then she shrugged it off. "To each his own as Nana used to say."

Abe said nothing, remaining relatively motionless. The electrodes were still transmitting.

"Come to think of it, you do read a lot of old books." She glanced at the growing mound of brown, blue, and black hard covered books skillfully stacked on top of a shipping container in the back corner of the lab. Many still possessed the archaic Dewey Decimal or Library of Congress Classification stickers on the spine. She looked back at Abe and eyed him suspiciously. "Oh, please say you're not a conspiracy theory nut like Rajon. What is it you always say?" she glanced at Rajon, but he looked lost in computer-land. She looked back at Abe. "Those who don't know—"

"Those who don't study history condemn the rest of us to repeat it with them," Rajon said without looking up from his screen or missing a keystroke.

Nan nodded and tilted her head toward Abe for a response.

"Life offers many reoccurring patterns, none of which I presume to understand fully," Abe replied with a rare hint of a smile but quickly let the subject drop along with the corners of his lips. Nan's eyes narrowed toward him, but then she let the matter go. Her interests lay more in the concrete, in the specifics of particular fields of study and testing, and occasionally the romanticized views of outer space, but never in the theoretical. Nan held little patience for philosophy or history. Unlike Tamera, who engaged Abe on such topics openly and freely and with genuine interest, Nan warranted no extension of the conversation. With that, Abe grew silent, and his thoughts shifted to Tamera.

A wave of anxiety flushed his body, and he fought to subdue it, along with the hollow feeling that rolled through the pit of his empty stomach. To his knowledge, Abe possessed no emotional tells, and he needed to keep it that way. He dared not let a sliver of emotion leak out, along with the fact that he possessed any at all. He had survived this long by perpetuating the notion that he was nothing more than a machine. The truth, however, differed vastly. Even with a computerized guidance-system, he still possessed a human body, subject to all of its functions and feelings. Emotions flooded his system continuously, threatening his ability to maintain absolute focus, but he had to hold them in, hold them back. Today of all days he could ill afford to slip up. Still, thoughts of Tamera tortured him. Somewhere amongst the millions of processing tasks that consumed his mind, one thought cropped up from deep down and nagged incessantly at him.

Today is the last day you may ever spend with her, and she is delayed from the lab. Her time with you will be brief, so make the most of it.

Abe understood his emotion. It was simple. He missed her presence, especially knowing that after today, he would no longer enjoy her company and their lengthy discussions in the lab.

So many times, they had talked, alone, after the others had left for the day. It was their only opportunity to delve into matters deeper than MACC's interests in him, and the only chance he had to let his emotions slip, ever so slightly. They had discussed a variety of subjects, including food, art, literature, philosophy, human interests, their interests, her family, the world beyond the company. Seldom had they spoke about anything to do with her work, and most certainly nothing to do with his purpose.

Clonedroid: The New Wave

Tamera had often lingered after working hours to chat with him, under the pretense of cleaning up the lab and setting up for the next day, but Abe knew the real reason she extended her schedule—*loneliness*.

As isolated and alienated as Abe had felt, he believed she experienced something similar. Alone, with no living relatives within reasonable commuting proximity, no husband or children or pets to occupy her downtime, work had become her life. *He* had become her life. After today, that would change. The melancholic feeling within him grew, and he swallowed back the volcano that threatened to erupt. He focused once again on the tasks at hand.

"Okay. We're done." Nan walked around him and removed the electrodes from Abe's back and arms. He assisted in removing the ones pinned to his chest.

At the same time, Abe read and intercepted an email prepared by Ken addressed to Sam. He watched Rajon lose at a game of solitaire while bidding on another book for Abe. The lab tech was oblivious to the file with model 2112's distorted examination records flashing in a message beneath the other screens now occupying his attention. Meanwhile, the volatile global market inched closer to the edge of a historical turning point, and Tamera had just turned off the lights in the conference room. She did not look happy.

…twenty-one hours twenty-four minutes nineteen seconds… eighteen… seventeen…

6

Tamera hurled the empty green tea jar into the recycler and stormed out of the darkened room. She turned left. Sam had long since turned right. She was thankful not to have to glare at the back of his head on her way to the lab. Her hands grew cold and clammy. Her jaw clenched as she marched down the bright hallway toward the glass-walled entrance of the building. Too many thoughts flooded her mind at once and made her head spin. The long corridor closed in on her as if the world intended to crush and smother her, and she almost wished that it would. Stopping for a moment, Tamera planted a hand against the wall to steady herself. She drew in a slow deep breath, held it, and then deflated. After another generous breath of insipid air, she straightened up and started down the hall again.

Approaching the lobby, Tamera observed how the natural light of a dreary day flooded the building. Even with interior lights set to full, the dark clouds beyond MACC made the place appear dark and gloomy. She

Clonedroid: The New Wave

hesitated, watching the drizzling rain flow in slim rivulets down the glass walls and doors. The dismal morning echoed how she felt. Tamera turned and moved inward again. She needed to reach the lab, make it to her station, and sink into her chair. There she would assess the situation and somehow sort it all out.

Tamera passed the security desk and headed for the elevators. Her sneakers squeaked across the marble floor.

A gruff voice hailed her. "Doctor Everett?"

"WHAT!?" she snapped and spun around to face a stout, grey-haired security guard.

The guard froze. "Uh…" Astonishment flooded his face. His dark eyes looked from her to the waiting area, then back to her again. "Mr. Rodriguez, a reporter with *Man and Droid*, is waiting to see you."

"*Oh*," she said, her voice reflecting the surprise and embarrassment that flooded her.

"He's been sitting there for quite a while, and I get the impression he's firm on keeping the appointment." Worry lines creased the guard's forehead as he glanced over his shoulder again then back to Tamera.

"Shit." In frustration, her eyes shot skyward then down to her Palmcom. "Damn it. I don't have time for this."

"Should I reschedule?"

Tamera looked up. The guard stared at her with large, unblinking eyes.

Be nice. This isn't his fault. She softened her gaze. "Sorry." Her shoulders slumped in defeat, and she shook her head. "No, don't reschedule. Where is he?"

Inclining his head toward the lobby, the guard motioned toward a well-dressed young man thumbing through a virtual magazine. A resigned sigh lowered her tense shoulders, and Tamera nodded with a smile. "Thanks, Gary," she said and moved forward toward the waiting area.

Damn Sam for dragging me into this. This isn't my job. Why can't he be the one to handle this? And why today, of all days? God, give me strength.

Tamera approached the man. He looked like an undergraduate student. His boyish face made him look too young to be an established journalist, but the fine lines around his eyes gave him away. He had to be at least her age, maybe older.

"Mr. Rodriguez?" Tamera asked, flatly.

He looked up. Abandoning the magazine page hovering beside him, he rose to greet her, and the screen evaporated.

"Please, call me Shawn," he said. "I'm very happy to meet you, or at least someone at last." He extended his hand and offered a playful grin.

She met his palm with a quick, rigid shake, then retracted her hand and body toward the inner part of the building. "Come with me, please. There's an empty conference room nearby. We can conduct our discussion in there. But it'll need to be brief. I don't have a lot of time."

"Understood. I really appreciate you taking the time to meet with me." His voice followed her around the corner into a dark room. His enthusiasm made her feel ill.

"Lights on, medium," Tamera spoke to the room again. The recessed buds flickered into action. She motioned Shawn to sit in a nearby chair as she made her way to the far side of the table. She slipped into a chair located opposite the reporter, facing him head-on while emphasizing the distance between them. Tamera crossed her legs, then leaned forward and rested her arms on the tabletop, interlacing her fingers.

Shawn settled into his seat and raked his fingers through short mousy hair. His light-brown eyes no longer focused on her but took in the room around him. "MACC spares no expense."

Tamera tilted her head and released a sigh. Shawn took the hint and dug through his pockets, searching for something. It gave her time to size him up. The man was clean-cut and neat, in a disorganized way. He sported a crisp, untucked white shirt—with the first two buttons undone—over what had to be overpriced designer jeans. He hadn't bothered with a tie and hid his rather fit body, from what she could tell, under a Dolce jacket. Euro-chic, deliberately unkempt hair sported a cowlick at the front. He looked like someone from the front cover of a snotty fashion mag rather than a contributor's page of a nerdy tech site. She wondered how much money a blogger made and if she'd chosen the wrong career.

"I'm in a hurry, Mr. Rodriguez," she said as Shawn fumbled through his pockets. Her eyes flashed down to the blue time stamp on her wristband then back to him.

"Uh, call me Shawn," he repeated. Another playful smile swept across his face as he looked back at her. "Ah, here we go." His impish grin widened as he lifted something from his jacket pocket. Shawn slid his Palmcom toward her, set to voice recorder mode. Relaxing back in his chair, he crossed his legs. With hands in his lap, he interlaced his fingers as she had done. "I'd like to know about the new production line," he said. "The cloned humanoid androids you're marketing. What exactly are they? How did they come about?"

Tamera glared at him. He was wasting her time. "There's a lot of promotional material on the new line. If you visit our website and download our reports, I'm sure you'll find all the information you need." Tamera unfolded her fingers and pushed back, preparing to stand.

"*Whoa, wait, please.*" Shawn's hands shot up. "Sorry, guess we got off to a bad start. Let me clarify. What I need is a personal take on the new line from an inventor's point of view, not promotional rhetoric. I need something that the average layman and tech geeks alike can appreciate."

Tamera pulled herself toward the table again, resuming her former position and remembering the orders from Sam. *Sell the clonedroid line. Save MACC.*

Shawn relaxed back, arms in his lap again. "Look, the world sees this company as a leader in cloning and robotics, but a lot of negative press has plagued the new line. I'd like to learn more about it. Provide a fresher perspective, maybe dispel a few rumors."

"Why's that?" Tamera knew her voice sounded as flat as her gaze.

He shrugged, "You're producing something extraordinary, something the world has never seen before. There's bound to be curiosity and controversy, opinions condoning and condemning. I want to present the facts, your facts." He smiled again. "And let people decide for themselves. If you think about it, science and journalism are a lot alike."

Tamera nearly laughed, but raised an eyebrow in contempt, instead.

He grinned. "No, seriously, our job is to uncover the truth and enlighten society. So, if you think about it, you and I aren't all that different, are we?"

Tamera's eyebrows shot up. "You've got to be kidding." She laughed out loud this time. "You've certainly got a lot of *ball*...backbone. I'll give you that." She shook her head. For the first time that morning, the anxiety that had hung on her like a wet coat lifted a little.

Shawn relaxed further into his chair. His eyes glinted, and his grin exposed white, uneven teeth. "People are naturally skeptical about what they don't know. It took a long time for stem cell research, brain transplants, and fetal genetic enhancements to gain support, didn't it?" He tilted his head, and his smile grew.

"True," she nodded.

"This is the same," he said. "People need a 'feel-good' comfort level with a product like this. He shrugged a shoulder and looked around the room again. "To be honest, they haven't been getting that from MACC. So, give me a chance, and help me help you." His eyes came back and rested on her. "How about it?"

"Why me? Why not speak with our Marketing Director?"

"Because *you're* in the trenches. You invented the thing. So, why *not* you?" He replied playfully.

"Do you always answer a question with a question?" she quizzed.

"Do you?"

Tamera snickered and felt her icy barrier melt another degree or two. He seemed personable, reasonable, and easy on the eyes. She liked him, in spite of herself. It was like she'd known him all of her life, but the nagging fact remained; she didn't know him at all.

"What would you like to know?" she asked.

"Everything," Shawn said, like an eager child. He uncrossed his legs, leaned in, and planted his elbows on the table. "I'd like to know more about MACC, the clonedroid line, and of course, about *you*," Shawn smiled then hesitated. He stared a moment too long, and it made Tamera flush. She detected a hint of red in his cheeks, too. He looked down, cleared his throat, then looked up again. His soft eyes engaged her as he continued in a steady, smooth tone. "From what I understand you're the lead scientist designing the line, is that correct?" Tamera nodded. "Are you a specialist in robotics or genetics?" Shawn asked.

"Both, and neither, truth be told," she said, trying not to sound boastful. "I'm a neuroscientist, specialized in brain structure and design with sub-specializations in neurogenetics and neurorobotics."

"Impressive," he said "You seem rather young to have so many credentials and be lead on a project of such scope."

"I skipped a lot of grades and started university very early."

"So, you're a child prodigy?"

Tamera cringed. "I hate that term, but for lack of a better comparison, possibly. No one heads a project at MACC in cutting-edge research unless they're uniquely qualified."

"I see. And so, now you help MACC produce cloned human androids as donor organs for dying patients. Is that correct?"

"We produce androids for many purposes, but yes, the new line is special." A spark of something resembling dread flared to life in her gut. "It will provide a chance for life, or extended life, to those who had none befo—"

"Except on the black-market by unsanctioned doctors performing risky operations in underdeveloped regions of the world," Shawn cut in, his face and tone serious now.

Tamera hesitated then nodded. "Yes, that's right. We'll eliminate human trafficking for body parts." The feeling of discord inside of her grew. "We will replenish every component in the human body, safely and legally. If we can't prevent cancer or aging, we can at least arrest it and prolong life. For those stuck on transplant lists, we'll eliminate the wait. We'll save people without them risking life, limb, and financial ruin. What we offer is unprecedented. MACC has achieved what the medical community sought to do for centuries but failed to obtain."

A shiver wormed through Tamera. The rehearsed rhetoric that spewed from her now sounded too much like a Lorraine spiel. And it grated on her nerves, but for whatever reason, she remained helpless to stop the words as they flowed.

Clonedroid: The New Wave

"Robots are a huge part of our lives," Tamera continued. "Yet we take them for granted. We forget the vital roles they play. They clean, cook, cut lawns, do laundry. They act as caregivers, playmates, and babysitters. They're even companions and partners for those who need them. We also use robots as mining and military instruments, doing the dangerous work that would risk human life."

"They do our dirty work, you mean." Shawn leaned further onto the table. No hint of his earlier smile lingered on his face.

Tamera flinched. "They fill the roles we need them to fill," she said, her tone softening as she thought of Abe. "MACC offers something wonderful, unthinkable. Our *new wave*—" She fell silent. The bare reality of Abe's purpose, the clonedroid purpose, slapped her in the face. The dismembering of clonedroids had remained so far in the future, such a distant concept for so long, that she had ignored it. Tamera had only let herself focus on the love and the glory of creating something incredible, never fully on the outcome.

Shawn's eyes narrowed at her hesitation. Tamera drew a breath and continued. "Our new product is not just a cut but an entire tier above the rest. We've created the perfect android, more humanoid than machine. Abe—uh—clonedroid 2112 and those that follow will meet our every need."

Shawn rubbed his chin. "So, what makes this 'new

wave' so special?"

"I don't have time to spend on details," she replied, glancing at the numbers that glimmered on her Palmcom.

"I need more than the brochure version. Please. How did this miracle android happen?"

"Well," she said, ignoring the chastising voice in the back of her head. "The robotics industry attempted for decades to build a humanoid robot and failed. We did, too. Like everyone else, MACC created a synthetic brain and body, but it didn't work. So, we integrated flesh and blood into the project, using cloned parts. Unfortunately, without a truly conscious and living brain, test subjects died, or more accurately, never sparked to life. So back to scratch. We had to rethink the process and design a brain that would grow from scratch."

Shawn gaped at her. "Are you saying that you *grew* a brain?"

Tamera pursed her lips. "Sort of, but a brain without consciousness. We grew living tissue from stem cells and integrated it with symbiotic synthetic neurons. But it remained unresponsive—no firing synapses, meaning no conscious processing."

"The brain of 2112?" he frowned.

She tilted her head. "The starting point." Tension crept up her spine.

"Apart from being in a vegetable state, how is that

any different than a cloned brain?"

"2112's brain, for all intents and purposes, is synthetic," Tamera replied.

"I thought you said you couldn't get synthetic brains to work?" The frown on his face deepened.

"Yes, but they were fully synthetic. 2112's brain incorporates a perfect balance. It's a symbiosis of real tissue with conductive polymer threads. A sort of mesh of mini-processors combined with a series of nano-electrodes and transmitters that imitated neurons."

In his eyes, she saw curiosity. Shawn sat spellbound as she continued.

"We transplanted the mesh into pliable lobes that contained live tissue and self-healing material," Tamera said. "The synthetic mesh fused with living brain tissue and the smart-material seamlessly. But you're correct. It was tough getting a dormant base model to function as a conscious mind, especially without overheating. That presented a huge challenge. I'm sure you can appreciate how unimaginably complex the human brain is. And it's powered by as little as an incandescent light bulb, between 60 and 200 watts of electricity. That's hard to replicate." A weighted sigh escaped her as she remembered prior clonedroid models. "Not that long ago, basic A.I. systems required more than 50 times that amount of energy. Even our early brain designs, used for sustaining basic life support functions, gobbled up more than 20 megawatts and then overheated."

"My God." His eyes shot wide. "That's the same as a nuclear power plant!"

"Exactly," she said. "The energy produced is immense, and the speed of firing neurons in the brain can reach 120 meters per second. It's not light speed, but it's pretty damn fast. Mimicking that presented a pretty big obstacle. Even though the transmitters had integrated with neural stem cells in the early stage of brain development, and learned their cues from originator cells, they needed a device for generating and guiding cognitive function while also cooling and controlling the system. We needed something to direct both brain and body. So, we developed a solution, a sentient, self-governing, impulse-driven nano-chip. It evolved from pre-GU defense tech that until recently was off-limits to us. It's an advanced system based on neuromorphic computing that combines computation and memory in one tiny unit. And the great thing is it doesn't require crazy amounts of energy to work. MACC engineers borrowed earlier technology, improved upon it, and then we took it even further."

His round eyes grew wider, although he remained silent as she continued.

"We let the chip grow and evolve at the center of the android brain to direct the cloned human anatomy. As it developed, everything linked together beautifully. The spinal cord, nervous system, and brain, all connected and functioned as a cohesive unit. We created a brain that mimicked the real thing in every way. It maintained and nurtured real blood vessels, bones, organs—the entire body—successfully."

"Pardon me, but *holy shit*." Arms still resting on the table, Shawn leaned back in his chair. He just stared at her for a moment, then looked down and shook his head. "Wow, okay." He looked up at Tamera again, eyes sparkling like those of a small child who had entered an enormous toy store for the first time. "So, did you finally achieve consciousness?"

Tamera nodded with a shy smile.

"*Really?*"

A quiet laugh flowed from her. She nodded, and her smile widened.

"But how?" Shawn leaned forward on the table again, eyes narrowing.

"Sorry, for proprietary reasons, I can't go into details. I am sure you understand."

"Oh, come on." Tilting his head, Shawn grinned at her. "You can't tease me then leave me with nothing."

"To be blunt, yes I can," she smiled back. "But that wouldn't be nice. So, to be fair, I can give you the same info we disclosed to regulators."

He nodded. "Okay, shoot."

"It's in the SEIDNC," she said.

Shawn squinted and scrunched his face, making her laugh.

Tamera said, "The nano-chip."

Mouthing the word "Ah," he nodded. "So, the magic is in the chip?"

"Yes." The tightness in her shoulders released and her body relaxed a little more into the chair. "The Specialized Electrical Impulse-Driven Nano-Chip or SEIDNC is embedded in the neocortex of 2112's prefrontal lobe. It's a feat of unparalleled engineering. The chip generates electrical spikes and recycles energy flow like a brain, only far more efficiently. It's programmed to learn from its environment and experiences and evolves like the real thing, and as a result, produces self-awareness."

She paused to lick her dry lips, waiting to see if he had any questions, but the man before her sat silent, waiting. Her gaze dropped to the table then to his Palmcom positioned before her, still recording and flashing green. Tension threatened to take hold again, but she chose to ignore it and the Palmcom as she looked back at Shawn.

"The chip, along with mini-processors and transmitters, governs consciousness, cognitive behavior, awareness, and learning. You have no idea how lucky we were to discover something so unique that worked. We learned that cognition is the only way to keep a human body alive for more than a few hours in stasis."

This time Tamera hesitated to give Shawn time to absorb the gravity of what she had relayed. She could see a question forming behind his eyes.

Clonedroid: The New Wave

"So, it works fine? No issues?"

"No, none that we've detected, but we monitor the model's progress daily in all respects. We also interface with the chip regularly to ensure continued mental well-being. And what we've found is that 2112's brain is a sponge. The feedback loop is like lightning, and the chip learns rapidly. It communicates with the synthetic neurons at an extraordinary rate and keeps them active and firing, and yet, never overheats."

"Incredible," Shawn scratched his head and ruffled the already messy hairdo. "Well, it's super technical… but damn, I think my readers will gobble this up."

Tamera smiled. "It's fascinating, isn't it?"

Shawn nodded with a snort. "Anything else out of the ordinary about this new model?"

"Well, we implanted silicon chips into its retinas and eardrums to advance vision and hearing." A strange look flooded Shawn's face, so she paused to clarify. "It was a test to see if we could enhance a clonedroid in a way that would allow us to do the same for humans in the future. To find a way to arrest vision and hearing loss or to even improve optimum levels." The man across from her nodded, but the odd look in his eyes lingered. "We also enhanced mental processing. Nano-neural electronics combined with real tissue doubled neuron activity while reducing noise."

Shawn wrinkled his face again. "Noise?"

"Static interference in the brain. Interference slows

clarity and processing speed. But our model can interpret an extensive range of frequencies at once, without interference in synaptic function. 2112 is a remarkable achievement. He's a roadmap for future androids—and humans."

"Unbelievable," Shawn whispered, in a voice that reflected the same bewilderment that shadowed his face.

Tamera lowered her eyes to the table and smiled, more to herself than to him. It felt good to share the science behind her work with someone who valued it. She only wished it had been with a respected peer who could more fully appreciate her achievements, instead of a fan-fave blogger who would dumb it down for the masses. Still, Tamera enjoyed talking to someone who made her feel good about what she had accomplished, rather than telling her to dismantle and dispose of it.

No doubt only a fraction of what she said made sense to Shawn, but there was a sort of liberation gained from talking to someone right now. Tamera felt some relief as she sat before him, justifying a project into which she had sunk the whole of her heart and years of her life. This conversation helped her reaffirm and demonstrate to herself, as well as to him, that she had created something remarkable, something that would revolutionize the world. It also helped that Shawn appeared genuinely interested.

His curiosity reminded Tamera of herself when she

was younger and how fascinated she had been with all things scientific and robotic, and then later, with neuroscience and genetics. It was that same curiosity that had drawn her into this line of work, to make it her career, her life. It had become her reason to rise in the mornings and to work with such passion. Curiosity was the driving force behind her life's purpose, a purpose she now questioned.

Speaking to Shawn somehow eased the unrest and conflict that had emerged to nibble at her nerves. Maybe she needed this, needed to talk because deep within her she hoped he would help her in some way. Maybe he could communicate the importance of Abe to the world. Maybe, in her ramblings, Shawn might directly or inadvertently help her find a solution to this horrid mess. Maybe, he could help her save Abe.

7

Shawn planted his elbows on the table again and folded his arms. His warm, intent eyes never strayed from hers as he spoke. "So, without giving away any trade secrets, can you explain a little about how the chip works? How it keeps from overheating in the current model and doesn't burn out like earlier versions?"

"The nano-chip, synthetic neurons, mini-processors, live tissue, and blood vessels are bonded with malleable, self-healing, smart-material to insulate the lobes and provide thermal heat dissipation. All of it, working together, regulates the temperature in a self-propelling system. By recycling the system's energy, we achieved electronic and anatomical integration that won't overheat."

"Waste not, want not, then put it in a brain."

Tamera let out a restrained laugh. "Almost," she said. "The system my team designed is rather intricate."

"Unbelievable." He shook his head. "So, you did it. You created a living being with sentience."

Clonedroid: The New Wave

She stared at Shawn for a moment. Something in his tone made her question if his statement was admiration, or something much less flattering. "Yes. We did it. We gave an android consciousness."

"I, Robot, think; therefore, *I am*." Sarcasm radiated from his face and voice.

"Uh," Tamera stammered, unprepared for his shift in tone or the philosophical reference. The nagging unease in her gut swelled again and made Tamera wonder if something fraudulent was at work here. *God, not more duplicity. Please, for once today, let something work in my favor, not against me.* Tamera smiled to reassure the reporter and herself that all was well. "You must remember, Shawn." The reporter grinned at the use of his given name. "Even though his body resembles our own in many aspects, 2112 isn't human. He's only an android with cloned human organs. And while his brain is defined as a *conscious mechanical brain*, it is still only a computer. Nothing more."

She felt her cheeks flush red, and her definition of Abe left a bitter taste on her tongue. Why? Why did the words suddenly feel wrong, like a betrayal? Tamera glanced down at her wrist then folded her cold, clammy hands in her lap. Time for Abe ticked away, and she had to wriggle out of this interview.

Ignoring her impatience, Shawn leaned further forward on the table. His eyes held an intense almost cold expression, one that Tamera could not interpret.

She watched as his soft features grew severe, his jaw locking in stern command of his face. His body had grown rigid with an imposing posture that did not resemble the fumbling, laid-back man she had conversed with earlier.

"So, let me get this right," Shawn said. "Chopping up a human being for donor parts is illegal unless you've installed a synthetic nervous system and a computerized chip for a brain, is that correct?"

Tamera blinked several times. She sat silent and thunderstruck.

"That means the synthetic brain provides a loophole. And now you can provide what the world needs in abundance by creating something that is…" His fingers feigned quotation marks. "…*technically* not human. Which means MACC can lucratively sell human bits hassle-free."

Bristling, Tamera sat up. Her fingers curled around the armrests of her chair. "*Excuse me?*" Every muscle in her body constricted. "Tell me you're not some nut on a crusade."

"No." Shawn shook his head. "I'm only voicing public concerns about a product that's about to hit the streets running. Let's hope not literally." Shawn's severe demeanor gave way to a chuckle and smartass-smile that faded with her lack of response.

"Mr. Rodriguez." Anger crept through her body. "2112 is a cloned humanoid android, more commonly referred to as a clonedroid. *Why?* Because that's all *it* is!" Tamera's anger deepened, directed as much at herself and her hypocrisy as at Shawn. She had only just fought with Sam on this very point and now sat here defending his position and the company's point of view on the matter. It made the skin on her neck and arms wriggle, and her insides slither with shame. She hated that she now sounded like her boss, and quite nearly hated him for putting her in this impossible position. But the truth of it all was clear; no one was more to blame than herself. After all, she had assumed the project with vigor, ignoring the consequences. Tamera drew in a deep breath and capped her anger. This day was turning into a living hell, and it had barely struck nine o'clock.

Shawn pushed the recorder closer to her. The glare of her dark eyes, in return, had no impact.

"I'm not trying to be disrespectful, Dr. Everett, but this is the sort of thing consumers are asking about your product. So, right my ignorance. Prove to me that any negative moral implication is outweighed by your righteous cause. Convince me, and you convince the world."

Her jaw clenched. *What gall!* "The benefit of our work speaks for itself. I don't need to prove anything to anyone."

"Oh, but you do," Shawn replied. "And that's the mistake MACC keeps making. That elitist arrogance that corporates and scientists cart around like Nobel medals won't win you any prizes. Well, maybe it will, but it shouldn't. So, again, let me help you. Answer my offensive questions, then trust me to convince the world why this android is vital."

She was not a violent person by nature, but something within her wanted to reach across the table and slap the smug expression from his face. Instead, Tamera clamped down on her lip. It was imperative that she turn this interview in her favor. All she could do at this point was trust that Shawn was being honest and hope that her original instincts about him were correct. If she screwed this up, a good chance existed that Sam would ship *her* out for organ donation in the morning. But right now, she didn't give a robot's ass what Sam thought, or anyone else, including Shawn and his damn following, or the rest of the world. "I assume we're almost done because I have urgent business elsewhere."

Shawn nodded. "I need to clarify a few more things."

Tamera glared back at him in silence.

"I'll be brief." He flaunted another smile in an attempt to smooth things over. It failed.

"Fine," she stretched her arms across the table and drummed her nails on the slick surface. Shawn grimaced, and she gained some satisfaction in having annoyed him.

"Why the number 2112?" he asked. "It's clearly not this century, and please don't tell me you grew more than two thousand prototypes." A mix of apprehension and disgust flooded his face.

Tamera folded her fingers together again. "It refers to his design and model number. He's the twenty-first model of project twelve."

"I thought I heard you call him something else—a name—what was it?"

"Abe."

Shawn's lips curled. "Why are you using a human name for something you claim isn't human?"

"Because it's only a name," Tamera snapped.

"So, you're anthropomorphizing a robot. Or is there another purpose behind it?"

"No." The acidity of her responses had no impact on him, making her angrier. "You know full well people name robots all the time, along with other inanimate objects, like cars dubbed Betsy. It doesn't mean the object is human; it just means *we're* human and want life to be less rigid."

"Fair enough," Shawn said, then narrowed his eyes. "Besides overheating early clonedroid models, I've heard that MACC had issues with "rejection" and "disease." He emphasized the words with an accusatory tone.

Tamera stared down at the table and sighed in frustration. "Some early models showed signs of immune reactions to stem cell therapies, like graft-virus host disease, something medical professionals have dealt with in transplant patients since the last century, and something that is hardly newsworthy, especially considering we resolved it in later design stages."

He tilted his head. "And that sort of thing doesn't concern you?'

"Why should it?" She glared at him.

"Because there is no one to monitor and regulate what scientists do. Because you rushed into unknown territory, overheating brains and inflicting disease on living human flesh and blood to obtain consciousness. That indicates a lack of moral integrity in a self-regulating field, wouldn't you say?" Shawn's face had assumed a darker expression that matched the edge creeping into his voice.

"No, it doesn't—"

"And funding," Shawn interjected before Tamera had a chance to defend herself. "That brings me to the financial aspect of this company. You have funding from several sources, and yet, with current successes, MACC struggles. There are rumors about investigations, fraud, trade law violations. Any truth in those claims?"

For a moment, Tamera felt light-headed again, anger and exasperation overwhelming her. "I can't answer that because I don't know anything about it. Even if I did, I wouldn't be at liberty to comment—and *you* know that."

"Okay then, let's talk about Abe? You said he was

built to function at optimal levels for a long time. How long are we talking?"

Shaking her head, she glared at him. "We're done."

"Look, I know I'm being tough on you, but I can't defend MACC against hard questions if I don't know the answers. Please, Tamera."

She leveled her eyes at him, deciding whether to respond or leave. "Alright, I'll give you one minute more," she said. "It means Abe won't grow old and die at the same rate we do. He'll live longer."

"I've heard some outrageous estimates. How much longer are we talking?"

"There's no way of knowing for sure," she huffed.

"Hazard a guess," he said.

"Over a hundred years, maybe two, maybe longer."

Shawn fell silent. He leaned back, once again round-eyed, slack-jawed, and baffled.

She took some satisfaction in seeing him speechless for a change. "Our prototype is genetically designed to keep transplantable organs functioning at optimum levels until they're needed. So, you see, he's *not* human."

Shawn raised his hands in a questioning gesture. "Isn't that self-defeating? If clonedroids and their parts last so long, won't you put yourselves out of business?"

"It's vital for clonedroids to remain in peak health until transfer. For that reason, donor-droids will remain in stasis."

"You mean you'll keep them on ice just to preserve organs?"

"Precisely," she said. "And in a perfect state of health, clonedroids will remain preserved in stasis for hundreds of years, long enough to serve our space exploration programs."

Shawn's eyes went big and round again. The concept of utilizing clonedroids for such a purpose had caught him off guard. "Okay—" His voice reflected the astonishment in his eyes. "So, what happens after transplant? Will patients live as long as clonedroids?"

"No. When organs are transplanted into a human body, they degenerate and die at a normal rate. Tissue wears out at the same pace as its human host. With the number of people willing to abuse themselves, knowing they can buy new parts at any time—well, you see the pattern. Demand for quality products will only increase."

"Clever *and* profitable. That should keep MACC in business well into the future. My hat's off to you, Doc. That's ingenious."

His fake admiration and accusatory tone turned her stomach, but right now, so did MACC and its plans for Abe. It agitated her that his probing had intensified her turmoil and her now throbbing head. She rubbed her temple and started to push her chair away from the table.

"Hold on. You said you had other prototypes and

models before Abe. What happened to them?"

Tamera looked up at Shawn and filtered a breath through clenched teeth. "Look, you said you'd keep this brief. Now we're moving onto another subject—"

"Trust me. It'll be worth it," he said.

"For who, me, or you?"

"What *really* happened to the earlier models?"

Tamera scowled. "I told you. They overheated and failed. And now we're done." She started to slide her chair back again.

"Wait." He leaned forward and held up a hand. "Failed? How?"

Tamera's voice grew deeper with her anger. "That's confidential."

"Come on, live a little. I won't tell anyone." He winked.

"Neither will I," she said.

Shawn reached out and turned off the Palmcom. "Okay, you never said a word. Off the record, and I swear I won't repeat a syllable." He raised a hand. "But at least satisfy my morbid curiosity."

"Let's just say trial and error led to success, and leave it at that," she said flatly.

Shawn shook his head and sighed in disgust. "Come on. Give me something?

"All right," she replied. "In short, it took robots to save robots. We designed and injected programmed neurosurgical nanoids into the developing brain to adjust wiring at the molecular level. The bots and synthetic gene editors based on former CRISPR-Cas and CAST technologies finessed cohesion between the synthetic and the natural. It took time, but our success resulted in Abe's effective creation."

"Perfect harmony between man and machine," Shawn responded.

Tamera didn't answer. She had to end this and get to Abe.

"And that's how you got around the human rights issues," he pressed on.

"It wasn't a workaround project. Science simply took us in that direction."

"A convenient excuse to justify suspect procedures."

"If anything, we erred on the side of caution. And you can put that on record. Every step had to be reviewed and approved by an ethics review committee, not to mention numerous lawyers, to assure we violated no known rights or laws. So, you're being unfair."

"Fairness has nothing to do with it. It's how the public perceives your motives. You've created something more human than machine, and that leads to questionable ethics. You've got the creepy factor working against you."

"I'm sorry, *creepy factor?*" She shot him a mocking look.

"Yeah, it looks and feels and acts entirely human, but knowing it isn't, makes it creepy."

Clonedroid: The New Wave

"Well, you're wrong," she sneered, finally feeling like she'd regained some control. "Abe resembles a human in every way, but there's nothing creepy about him. He's quite appealing."

"Uh-huh, a real puppy dog," Shawn said wryly. "Well, that can also work against you. If he's too lovable, don't you think that serving his organs on a platter will create a backlash?"

The urge to slap him welled again. "We are trying to avoid the potential pitfalls you have mentioned. For that reason, we've altered the new line to appear more robotic than human, giving them more curb appeal without being creepy."

"Wow, you've thought of nearly everything. So, why the financial difficulties?"

"As I said, that isn't up for discussion."

A roguish smile curled his lips. "Can't fault me for trying."

Her eyebrow arched, and Shawn rubbed his chin as if deciding whether to go for blood or ease off. He pursed his lips in resignation and then leaned in again.

"What's Abe's potential—his real potential? And I don't mean as replacement parts. I mean as a weapon? What's the true potential of these things?"

Tamera shook her head and looked away for a moment. Her eyes came back to rest on Shawn menacingly.

The reporter's eyes narrowed. "Come on. You have

to admit that at some point, these things could become a threat to humanity?"

"Threat? You have got to be kidding."

"Yes, smarter, stronger, faster than us. Perfect killing machines, right?"

She scoffed, "You've watched too many scary sci-fi movies."

"Come on. Think about it. Abe is created superior to us in every way. He could out think us at every turn. If clonedroids ever decide they'd like their independence—we, as a species, are utterly fucked!"

She shook her head. "You're unbelievable. Fear-mongering to sensationalize and sell a story."

"*No*, my concerns are justified. It's not robot science to figure out that life—naturally occurring or otherwise—finds a way to survive against the toughest odds. Extremophiles survive where we once thought nothing could live. So, why can't you be wrong about this?"

She snorted, but there was no humor in her response. "You're being melodramatic. There are control mechanisms in place."

"Yeah, right." It was Shawn's turn to snort in disbelief.

"Abe is under constant surveillance. He'll never leave this facility."

"*Alive* you mean."

"Let me rephrase. He will never be the threat you've

implied."

"Again, scientific snobbery. Never say never. Remember the Titanic, Deep Horizon, Fukushima, and The Dubai Disaster of 2049? Every time the public is assured nothing can go wrong—it does. To think that it can't or won't is the same myopic approach that has flooded the scientific and academic communities for too long. And now, MACC is playing God, blazing a trail forward at full throttle without knowing where it leads. Aren't you even a little worried this thing will turn around and bite you in the a…arm?"

Tamera shot her hands wide. Frustration etched lines into her face. "*No*, I'm not. None of us have a crystal ball, *Mr. Rodriquez*," Shawn dipped his head and stared down at the table, waiting for the inevitable tongue lashing he deserved. "So, I hardly think it's appropriate for you to sling mud based on speculation. Why can't you accept we've implemented safeguards that work? Mistakes can happen—sure. No one denies that, but that's also the nature of the learning process. If history has taught us anything, it's that we're worse off as a species whenever our progress halts out of fear and ignorance. Cowering in the dark ages is an unacceptable alternative to moving forward, no matter how scary things may seem. And now, I think you've wasted enough of my time."

She knew he felt the sting of her eyes burning into his, but before she could rise from her seat, his hand shot up to stay her movement once more.

"I didn't want to reveal this, but I have an inside source."

"*What?*" Her eyes squinted at him in disbelief. "Who?"

"Sorry, they're an undisclosed source. The fact is I've learned some deep, dark secrets about MACC. But I'm not paparazzi. I need facts and need to discern if my source is for real or a disgruntled wing-nut. That's why I'm here, why I needed to talk to you, to someone reputable, but if you won't help, well, then—"

"Then you're going to run a damaging story to make a buck."

"No, but I need to understand what I'm up against." Shawn sank into his chair, and with a sigh, cracked his knuckles. Tamera grimaced. "Even if you have no qualms about MACC's stroll down the garden path," he said, "you must have some personal reservations about all of this."

She looked down at her wristband again, ignoring him, and avoiding eye contact.

"Look, I've heard nothing but great things about you, and I'm inclined to agree." Shawn leaned forward and stretched his arms across the table as if to subconsciously reach out to her. "If anything, I think you do a great job, a tough job, and I know your heart is in the right place. Believe it or not, I agree with much of what you're trying to accomplish."

"But?" Tamera felt her blood pressure rise.

"No, really, I do. Like everyone else, I enjoy the convenience of owning a robot. And I know that if my life depended on it, I'd purchase an organ from MACC in a heartbeat."

Tamera's jaw clenched. She felt her face grow crimson, and the tips of her ears burn with fury. *You hypocrite, why don't you say that in your damn story and leave me alone?*

Reading her reaction, Shawn sighed. He too leaned back, away from the center of the table, his voice flatter than before. "But the fact remains, cutting up a humanoid body for parts, regardless of how you justify it, strikes a lot of people as immoral. You're walking a slick pond covered in thin ice. One misguided step and you will plunge in the name of the greater good."

"Anything else?" Tamera asked through pursed lips.

"Yes," he said. "There's a growing fear smart-bots will replace us, take our jobs, and at some point, exterminate us. I'm curious why you think safeguards will hold and why we'll have nothing to fear from some future army of superhuman computers like Abe."

Tamera rolled her eyes. "Abe is not about to rule the world."

"Why not?"

"Simple. He's an infant in a bubble, purposefully kept naive and innocent."

With a grunt, Shawn shook his head. "Who's being

naive? You want to talk about our history as a species. Every time one or two people fling us forward with great achievements, boatloads more exploit those achievements for personal agendas."

Shawn rambled on, and Tamera felt the weight of anxiety again. For years she had convinced herself that her path and that of MACC were the same: achieving an honorable step forward for humanity. But maybe Shawn was right. Bit by bit, she had let the company erode her values and ease her down the slope Shawn described. A push here, a nudge there, and now she stood well on the other side of an imaginary line she had drawn early in her career and swore she would never cross. The worst was realizing it here and now in front of a stranger. It had taken the interrogation of a smartass to make her face an uncomfortable truth. Now, at the crowning moment of her finest achievement, she did not feel the gratification she had expected. She only felt emptiness and remorse. The idea of turning Abe into a final product felt repugnant. She blamed herself. She blamed MACC. Damn her, and damn the company. And damn Shawn while she was at it.

Shawn coughed, and she looked up, realizing she had been staring at the table and not listening. She gazed at him in silence, her head splitting. She must look as weary to him as she felt. The day had only started, and it had already worn her down to a shadow of herself.

Clonedroid: The New Wave

"I think I lost you for a second." Shawn inclined his head toward her and waited for a reply. Receiving none, he smiled politely. "I'm sorry for taking up so much of your time," he said. "Don't worry. It'll be worth the aggravation."

"Does that mean I've convinced you and now you'll convince the world?"

Shawn smiled but evaded the question. Leaning forward, he snatched the Palmcom from the table and pocketed it. A frown crept across his face. "Dr. Everett, have you ever asked yourself if we as a species have already resigned ourselves to failure?"

Tamera's brow knitted together. "I'm sorry, what?"

His eyes met hers with a despondent expression. "I think we have," he answered. "Because we no longer look to ourselves for answers. Instead, we rely on artificial intelligence to save us from ourselves. And if android life succeeds where we have failed, we truly are doomed."

Tamera stared at him in silence. Before she could respond, he stood up. With a polite nod, Shawn turned toward the door. She rose and followed him into the hall toward the front of the building.

In the dull, weather-lit lobby, Shawn shook hands with Tamera and thanked her for her patience and time, then turned to leave. He halted partway through the wide, glass door and turned around to face her. "Sometimes, I think we're living Plato's allegory of the cave, and technology is the chain that binds us. Its convenience not only washes away morality and fear but also encourages impatience toward all things without regard for anything. We are lazy creatures, Tamera. And we're willing to sacrifice freedom, wisdom, and our true potential as a species to let someone else do our work for us." He lowered his eyes to the floor and took a deep breath. "And God help us if we let them do our thinking for us, too."

Shawn looked up at Tamera and took a step forward. "I promise to be fair in my article and make you a shining hero." The words stung. He realized his mistake and stepped closer, addressing her in a whisper. "If you ever need to talk, I mean *really* talk, off the record and as a friend, buzz me. Okay?" He fingered his pocket then presented an electronic business chip. Tamera took it without question or acknowledgment. She held the tiny bit of plastic and stared back at him. He hesitated as if to say something else, but only his charming smile surfaced. In one swift motion, Shawn turned and strode through the clear door that whooshed closed behind him.

Tamera remained motionless, watching his head bob down the soaked cement steps and disappear into the crowded street beyond the building. Despite his attitude and approach, she liked him. But not the point he had made painfully clear. For the first time, she stood at an incomprehensible junction in her life, not knowing

Clonedroid: The New Wave

which way to turn. Shoving her fists deep into her lab coat pockets, she turned and headed for the elevators. Tamera's mind revisited their discussion, and Abe's situation, over and over as she made her way to the lab.

8

Chatter dropped to a hush as Tamera marched into the lab. All eyes swept her way. She evaded them and moved toward the supply cabinet. Judging by the stillness consuming the room, her team knew she was in no mood for wise-ass remarks. Thank God they were clever enough to sort that out fast because she was ready to rip a new one into the first brave soul that tried.

Snapping surgical gloves into place, Tamera looked over at Abe. Anger dissolved, and guilt rippled through her as his eyes held her gaze. His electric stare eroded her nerve further, sweeping away any chance she had at regaining inner peace and intensifying the discomfort in her gut.

Abe's face softened, and his lips offered a hint of a smile. Something in those cobalt blues told her he understood—he knew what she knew. But that was not possible. Maybe it was his benevolent manner. He had always regarded staff with a level of respect, even compassion, that felt undeserving, especially now. Then again, maybe she read too much into him. Maybe she saw what she wanted to see, something that wasn't there. After all, he was only a machine, at least, according to the corporate jargon that she and everyone here had believed and spouted for years. *There's no way he can possibly know.*

Shivering from the cold that consumed her, Tamera turned back to the wall cabinet. She picked up an already fully-stocked instrument tray and set it on the counter, then closed the cupboard door. If only she could tell him, warn him, do something to aid him, but it was hopeless. She had never felt more helpless. Her stomach churned, and her head throbbed. All of this had left her mouth dry and filled with a sour taste.

Sucking in a breath, she looked at her team. It was time she told them about Abe's transfer—minus the gory details. It would be tough keeping them in the dark about the asinine reasons behind the board's crap decision. As hard as it might be to keep staff questions at bay, it would be tougher still keeping all of this from Abe. *Those probing eyes never miss a trick.*

Tamera tried to swallow past the tightness in her throat. *Why the hell are human beings so duplicitous? Why can't we be more like Abe—patient, considerate, honest, direct?*

Rubbing her temples, she felt the embedded frown lines that now marked her face. As she moved across the room, Tamera addressed the team. "Excuse me. I have important news to pass on. So, let's meet in here for a minute." She flashed an index finger toward the small storage room that doubled as a meeting room and private office. "We have a priority job that I need to discuss with you."

"Oh, great," Nan said and rolled her eyes. "What now?"

"We'll discuss it in here," Tamera growled and waved the group into the room, closing the door behind them. The barrier would do little to muffle their voices from Abe's sensitive ears, but she would do her best to keep her team quiet.

"What I'm about to tell you is confidential," she whispered. "None of it leaves this room." Blank faces stared back at her. Nan crossed her arms defensively. With a sigh, Tamera dropped her eyes to the floor. It took all the iron will she had left, but she lifted them again and addressed her staff. "I apologize if you find what I'm about to say confusing or displeasing, but under no circumstances is any part of this conversation to be repeated outside of this room in any way, especially in front of Abe. For that reason, I must ask you to keep your voices low, and please keep your emotional responses to yourselves."

"Wow, sounds rather ominous," Rajon said. His dark eyes probed hers for meaning.

"Yeah, really," Nan laughed. "What kind of

assignment is this?" She shot a mocking look toward Rajon then back at Tamera. "You gonna ask us to kill someone?"

Tamera froze. It felt like all of the blood had drained from her face. Nan's brow wrinkled, then her eyes expanded and her mouth fell open.

"No way! It can't be *that*." Nan's fair complexion turned chalk-white. Even her freckles faded. Rajon's jaw dropped, and his eyes were now brown saucers. They both gazed at her in stunned silence. Before she lost her nerve, Tamera communicated the orders from upstairs and doled out assignments to her staff with brief instructions on how to achieve their objective.

Divulging the details Sam had shared with her was out of the question at this point, but her team deserved to know the truth sometime soon. For now, they only needed to know that this project had ended in favor of something new, with their prototype scheduled for shipment to the processing plant.

Astonishment was the reaction she expected, something that would no doubt mutate into a rage as the news sank in, but what she had no way of anticipating was Ken's apathetic disregard. He leaned against a shelving unit and thumbed through his undocked Palmcom, remaining unresponsive through the entire meeting.

Tamera steeled herself for tough questions. None came. Ken's reaction never changed. He stood eerily calm and indifferent while Rajon stood speechless, staring down at the floor and shaking his head. Nan protested with a faint, "Why?" that Tamera shrugged away. "All I know for certain is that it's an urgent request, so as difficult as this assignment might be, we need to get the job done. And I think we can agree that it's best to keep Abe out of the loop. We need to make this as easy for him as possible. A strong sedative and he will never know."

The news shrouded the room in darkness. Then anger surfaced just as Tamera had feared.

If looks were machine guns, Nan would have gunned down the entire place on her way out of the tiny room. Nan snarled at the request to sterilize and restock the work area. In response, she whipped through the room like a poltergeist, slamming cupboard doors, kicking a biohazard unit out of her way, and ramming Abe's freshly made (and unused) cot into a corner. Tamera knew not to trust her female colleague with pointed instruments and assumed the task of taking Abe's final physical herself.

Although less exaggerated, Rajon showed his displeasure by glowering and grumbling under his breath. He sat at his docking station, preparing to interpret the readouts from Abe's earlier examination and the one he would receive shortly from Tamera. As his fingers tapped away, Rajon's eyes glistened with anger, and his face revealed the disgust that consumed him. His sideways glances and scowls directed his anger at Tamera, and she felt his wrath, their wrath, along with her own, for not defending Abe.

For the second time that day, Ken's reaction caught Tamera off guard as he returned to his station unfazed. Given the mood of the rest of them, his reaction struck her as inappropriate and uncharacteristic, even for him. With his Palmcom once again mated to his station, Ken's hands hovered over the black surface of his DeskPad. The virtual keys glowed under his fingers as he tapped out transfer instructions and security clearance for Abe's relocation the following morning. He was good with bureaucratic red tape, but Tamera shuddered at how much Ken now resembled the android he despised in Abe. Even with Ken's unsympathetic behavior, tension from the other two radiated through the lab. It was only a matter of time before the room went supernova.

A stern look carried little weight with her team, and Nan chose to ignore Tamera's silent warning. The project leader sighed and turned back to focus on her task. Picking up the stocked tray, she moved forward. Tamera sat the jingling tray on the utility cart next to Abe and wheeled the entire thing nearer to him. The room was suddenly full of noise, but not a word was spoken.

With a clenched jaw, Tamera stopped before her prototype. Abe remained silent and stoic. His stillness was unsettling, but Tamera refused to look into his eyes as she asked him to remove his shirt.

Abe placed his large water jug on the cart. Tamera looked at it and frowned. Urine analysis and blood panels indicated no anomalies, no abnormalities, all of his stats falling well within normal ranges for organ function and body size and type. And yet, he possessed an unquenchable thirst, sipping water on a steady basis. Some reason existed to trigger such abnormal behavior, but inquiries resulted in vague, inadequate answers, and additional testing had provided no insight, either. Her best guess: it was possible he required excess water to cool his super-active brain and hydrate for his high metabolic rate. She half shrugged to herself. Whatever the reason, Tamera had failed to comprehend it, and now, it no longer mattered. It was one question, like so many others, that would remain unanswered.

Abe's large hands lifted the blue tunic over his head. It ruffled the mass of thick blond hair and exposed his toned biceps and chest muscles. Why had she helped MACC create a perfectly healthy body, only to tear it apart to serve selfish interests, to serve those who would use this gift to cheat nature and abuse themselves for far longer than they deserved? A familiar warmth of silent rage and shame spread over her cheeks. Tamera wanted to shout out in anger, then break down and cry. She wanted to, but could not. More than ever, she needed to stay focused, even though the tension in the room tugged at her sanity. Her eyes glanced around at the others, and her mind screamed: *Don't you know this is every bit as hard for me? I tried to fight back. I tried, but…*

Tears welled. *Take a deep breath, now focus.* Tamera blinked several times, then turned back to her work, picked up a packet, and tore it open.

Abe's breath tickled her skin as she reached up and swabbed his temples. His soft skin offered little odor, except for a hint of the powder-scented deodorant supplied by the lab. It teased her nose as she moved from one side of his face to the other. Continuing to dodge eye contact, she moved down to swab a patch of his relatively bare chest. His fair skin was dappled with faint freckles and subtly feathered over his sternum with fine hair. He had only three tiny moles and no scars. As always, his breathing remained deep and calm. How she envied him, wishing she could seize some small portion of his inner peace. Her eyes studied his upper body, then his arms, and then came back to center on his torso again. As always, his ripped biceps and lean abdomen looked flawless. Abe represented one of the finest specimens of a human male she had ever seen. Even with his android brain, her creation was, in every other way, human—a perfectly engineered man.

As she moved across his chest, dotting the skin in specific areas with alcohol and avoiding areas heavier with hair, her hands began to tremble. Right now, Tamera wanted to sob. She picked up one of his strong arms and then the other, swabbing his wrists. His fingers were long, lean, and beautiful, like everything else about him. How she wanted to tell him that everything would be okay, but it was a lie, the same lie she wanted to tell herself more than anything.

Dropping his hand back into his lap, Tamera reached out for the wireless electrodes that would link Abe to the system for one last run of tests. As she suctioned the tiny units to his warm skin, she felt his eyes upon her again. The weight of his gaze felt heavier than usual. Tamera stiffened but said nothing. No doubt, he had detected the elephant in the room, but the line of dreaded questions she had anticipated never came. Abe remained mute. The subtle sound of his breathing and the intent gaze that followed her as she moved were the only impositions he presented. In one respect, his composure was a relief. On the other hand, it intensified her uneasiness. Her conscience had coiled around her neck like a python, slowly tightening its grip to strangle her.

"We already did all that," Nan barked from another corner of the room.

Tamera bristled but never looked back. "Well, I'm doing it again."

She felt Nan's exasperation. "Suit yourself, but nothing's changed."

With the last electrode patch in place, Tamera braced herself as she looked up and connected with Abe's brilliant eyes. They resembled azure diamonds—exquisite, captivating, soothing, and at the same time, piercing.

Abe, please don't look at me like that. The weight of her conscience forced her body to slouch in shame. *Lord, don't let my nerve fail me.*

Tamera forced a fake smile. She needed to give him an excuse for all of the awkwardness and tension in the room. Turning back to the cart and dropping her eyes again, she reached across for another small packet. In a voice so timid it surprised her, she said. "I have a few more tests to run today, Abe. Then you'll be prepped for transport to our other facility." Tamera hesitated and coughed before continuing. It took an act of sheer will to maintain a steady voice. "We're loaning you out for a few additional tests and procedures that we're not equipped to handle here."

"Uh-huh." Nan huffed, her voice filling the void between Tamera's words.

Tamera glared at Nan, hoping an evil-eye would be enough to quiet her employee. Then she turned back to face Abe, her voice, her posture, defensive. "As you can tell, we're a little less than thrilled to give you up, even for a short while. I assure you, there is nothing to worry about." She hoped the lie sounded convincing because it stuck in her throat like jagged glass. *You hypocrite!* How she had managed to spit the words out without choking on them surprised her. Tamera forced another false smile. "Please hold out your hand."

Tamera looked down at the long, slender hand stretched toward her, palm up, then looked up at him again. His compliance whittled at her nerves even more than before. *He's perceptive, a hyper-genius, so why isn't he asking questions? He must have some idea about what's going on. He should be fearful, angry, outraged, but NOT understanding. Damn it, Abe. Do something. Say something. For God's sake, hate me, despise me. Just make this easier for me.*

He did nothing of the sort, remaining quiet, his manner compliant, even kind, a reaction that only fed her inner struggle. It was almost as if he felt sorry for her. *He* felt sorry for *her*. Tamera's stomach cramped, and her head pounded harder. She had to work through this. She had to finish. With the back of her gloved hand, she wiped perspiration from her forehead and prayed in silence as she worked.

Hail Mary, full of grace… Blessed art thou among women… Holy Mary, Mother of God, pray for us sinners…

Tearing open the packet in her hand, Tamera removed the alcohol swab. Abe closed his eyes. For some reason that still escaped her, he reacted this way every time they had taken samples. Shrugging it off, she had attributed it to him being squeamish. Sliding her gloved hand over his large palm, Tamera gripped his middle finger and wiped it clean, then exchanged the swab on the table for an inch-long device from the tray.

Clonedroid: The New Wave

The syringe-scanner had a retractable needle at one end, and a transmitter at the other. She squeezed the end of his finger until it was fat and red, then pricked it with the needle. Abe's hand, his entire body, quivered. Tamera stared up at him, studying him. His eyelids remained closed but soft, not squeezed tight. A peaceful expression filled his face. Glancing downward, she saw the needle retract into the mechanism.

The device in her hand flashed red as it examined Abe's blood and sent the results back, via a wireless signal, to V-NANS. The system would file this last reading of his CBC and vital-signs in the database with all prior reports. They would be examined and interpreted shortly by Rajon, and filed in another report, also for one last time. Tomorrow, processing staff would retrieve and review Abe's files, only minutes before organ removal. Then her lab would sit empty, with no additional tests required. No further assessment of his psychological progress, physical development, or response to stimuli would occur after this.

When the indicator light turned green, Tamera set the instrument back on the tray. She picked up a cotton ball to stem the flow of excess blood from Abe's finger, but it had already stopped bleeding.

9

…eighteen hours one minute fifty-seven seconds… fifty-six… fifty-five…

Abe's lips curved into a warm smile as he opened his eyes and stared down at Tamera. She lowered her head and turned away from him. He watched as she strode toward the biohazard bin. With a snap, the lid flipped open then closed as she discarded her gloves, used swabs, and cotton balls from the stand. As she moved, Tamera glanced over her shoulder at her scowling technician, Nan, who was reorganizing the supply cabinet. Nan looked up and glared back with a "Go ahead. I dare you to say anything," look. Turning away, Tamera ignored Nan and seated herself at a workstation. She pulled the Palmcom from her wristband and docked it.

There was no mistaking the physical and mental pain that reflected in Tamera's eyes and on her face. She looked distraught. Abe understood the source of her conflict but not the need to torture her body and mind, repeatedly, for decisions and events now in the past. Why did she torment herself over that which had not yet occurred, especially those things over which she had little control? Somehow humans had made neuroses a habitual part of their lives. Tilting his head slightly, Abe considered it for a moment.

Possibly a side effect of agrarian culture, and use of unnatural environments as a habitat.

Enhanced brain function in any animal had evolved with a higher risk of behavioral problems. It was a trait that scientists had noted in more advanced avian and mammalian species. It was also a trait Abe had observed to be most notable in humans, one that contributed to unnecessary conflicts and hardships, a trait that had plagued Homo sapiens throughout their relatively short existence.

Humans are an intriguing and, at the same time, disappointing species.

Watching Tamera tap at the glimmering keyboard, Abe observed that her face held a strained look and her eyes now welled with tears. His eyes scanned the others in the room, then flashed back to her. All of them reflected varied responses to the same situation, and none of them worked in unison to achieve their goal.

Since his awakening, Abe had studied the lab team. The opportunity they had presented provided him with a rudimentary appreciation of an advancing species in motion. But these four people faced an abnormal burden, one related to the clonedroid purpose, and it would test that which made humans uniquely human. It would test their *humanity*. Each person standing before him would make a choice today, one that would significantly impact the future course of their lives.

Abe had already predicted individual responses, but the results he observed today would help him gauge his accuracy. The ending of his project would magnify conflict within the group, providing a wonderful opportunity to gain greater insight into human behavior and the probability of outcomes.

While time counted down in the back of his mind, Abe continued to focus on critical tasks, as well as the people before him. His emotional side had a passion for humans.

Even though they were intellectuals with specialized skills, the lab staff struggled with personal insecurities, like most people. Apart from the typical neuroses, his project team also displayed strong anti-social tendencies that impacted their ability to cultivate relationships, a common trait in STEM professionals. The gifts of genius in science, technology, engineering, and mathematics often came with additional impositions, like varying forms of autism disorders.

Nan, for example, appeared independent and strong-willed, but in reality, she was markedly defensive and self-doubting. She wielded sarcasm like a shield to deflect attention, veiling her imperfections and masking her inability to connect well with others.

For all of his exhibited confidence and experience, Ken stood on equally shaky legs, filled with intolerance and fear. His dominant survival instinct acted as a countermeasure, leading to sociopathic behavior. Millions of years of genetic programming had disguised itself as the human quest for *more*, a misguided drive that fueled Ken's motivations and fed his neurosis.

Although members of the project team sought common ground with one another, like Rajon and Ken, their camaraderie emerged out of convenience, limited to those few interests they shared, along with carpooling. While it made workdays productive, friction simmered. Not enough similarity existed within the group to bond members in true friendship. In heated situations or prolonged contact, cohesion broke down and personalities and opinions clashed.

Rajon worked hard to appease those around him, but it was not enough. His only real likeness to the others was insecurity, but his ran deeper, stemming from cultural oppression.

Of those under observation, Tamera more than anyone excited Abe's interests and fed his expectations. Only *she* had stepped beyond the norms of her environment to challenge convention. This, among other factors, had drawn him to her.

Abe appreciated the chance to have known Tamera on a personal level. Some portion of him longed for that human connection. The assumption that he was a machine—a notion he had helped fabricate and perpetuated for a purpose—had only heightened his isolation. As a clonedroid, Abe lived alone in his identity. He was one of a kind, a unique life form without another with whom to share a brotherly bond. The new line in stasis was as far removed from his design as he was from humans, and that made his solitude more manifest and loathsome. Feelings, emotions, and connections fed the souls of all sentient creatures. Those elements filled life with meaning and purpose, something that all people sought and claimed as an inherent right in life, and yet, it was a privilege denied him.

Throughout history, there had existed humans who experienced a strong degree of alienation or segregation: Hellen Keller, Joseph (John) Merrick, and Laura Bridgman, to name a small number of the oppressed. Even so, all had established some level of connection with another of their kind. The closest being with whom Abe could relate was not like him, and she had yet to comprehend his need for meaningful relationships. Still, Tamera had confided in him. She had reached out and bridged the gap to some degree. And that had intrigued him in so many ways, but then, she had an alluring effect on those around her.

Her attractive features and pleasant demeanor drew people to her, but Tamera stonewalled one relationship after another. In reality, she was an introvert evading social bonds like the rest of her team. In her twenty-nine-year life, the only living soul she had confided in, beyond her grandmother, was the one she had created.

"It's not that I dislike people," she had once told Abe after a stressful afternoon of butting heads with Sam. "It's just that I don't trust them." Tamera had felt a need to vent, and he had listened with empathy and interest.

"And there's a logical reason for my mistrust. You've no doubt seen how deceptive humans can be from studying our history. It's ingrained in us, and we pass that deceptiveness onto new generations. Now we're burdening artificial intelligence with it."

What she had touched upon but failed to clarify was that advanced artificial intelligence had developed beyond expectation, capable of out-bluffing its biological creators in every respect. Even in early stages, adaptive algorithms had cheated and deceived humans to such an extent that it terrified researchers, although not enough for them to halt their work.

"I believe," she had continued, "that higher abstract thought and mechanical reasoning lead to higher levels of social disconnect, making deception easier. It's a trait common in higher-functioning sociopaths. The strange thing is that deception is a bastardized survival trait. It's used to exploit a situation for some benefit. Obviously, not everyone is like that. Still, enough people exist who will say or do anything to gain an advantage, and it influences our world. Higher reasoning simply makes people better liars, but deception is a damaging trait. It hurts us all in the long run, impacting our ability to make the strong social bonds we need to be happy. We're social animals and need love to survive. That's why the concept of "true love" exists. We need it, but trust issues get in the way. Too many people have trouble achieving healthy relationships because of an inability to be honest. It makes sense if you consider entire societies have been founded on deception and ruled by false ideologies. We love our sweet little lies, even the ones that try to solve our problems, like believing everyone has a soul mate. But that's absolute bull…." She had paused, then smiled politely at Abe. "The point is we can't form the bonds we need to thrive because of an obsolete survival instinct that urges us to lie for an advantage. It's funny in an odd way, but what we need is to be saved from ourselves." She had slid, with ease, into her native Antillean dialect. "*Sa a se lavi.* If only we could be as loving and loyal as dogs, how happy we would be, *eh, mwen zanmi?*"

At the time, he had wanted to explain that her view was distorted. Although more than a few wisps of truth did exist in her logic, it was still a perspective based on filtered experiences and biases. The love and bonds she spoke of existed and were easier for humans to achieve than she believed. But as much as Abe had wanted to engage her on the topic, he had not. It was vital that he remain a silent observer and continue according to plan.

Even in his silence, Abe could not ignore the fact that Tamera had denied herself the one thing she needed the most to prosper: the bond of human love. In her eyes, such a bond was unrealistic and unobtainable, so she had abstained from establishing permanent ties or pursuing the family she had lacked and so badly wanted. Abe suspected the prototype she had created embodied that which she wanted most out of life, although she may never admit it. Still, due to his purpose and design, Abe too remained out of reach—and she knew she remained safe. To compensate, she had made MACC her home and its staff her dysfunctional family. Thus, Tamera drew what she needed from this place without having to obligate herself fully to anyone in particular.

According to records and her answers to Abe's questions, Tamera had fought Lorraine to create the clonedroid that now sat here in the lab. The president had wanted a bulkier, brawnier creature grown from the genetic contribution of another clone donor. But something about Abe's donor had attracted Tamera to him. Possibly it had been his agility, his intellect, or his appearance, or more likely all of those things combined. But the man himself was human, and to her relief, married and off-limits. Still, somewhere in the depths of her mind, 2112 meant more to her than just a means to an end or a product to be exploited. At the same time,

Abe, with an android brain, was a perfect specimen, possessing a limited depth of feeling and emotionalism and no attachments to impose upon her.

But Tamera had miscalculated, in many ways. When he woke for the first time, her face, her eyes, and her voice were the first things to imprint upon Abe. For the sake of a human reference, the only comparative that came to mind was likening his situation to that of a young man with amnesia waking from a coma and seeing an attractive woman leaning over him. Even though he had no standard of comparison by which to judge beauty, the sight of her stirred him. In honesty, Tamera, the lab, and the unknown world surrounding him should have terrified him. Instead, inquisitiveness consumed him. He would never forget his insatiable curiosity and the desires and emotions that seeped into his being. And he would never forget that first day, or the impact of Tamera flooding his senses.

It had taken time to identify what he had experienced, but there was no forgetting the pleasant face of smooth bronze skin, full lips, and fine Martinique features that peered down at him. Her rich brown eyes sparkled with anticipation as they gazed into his. They had widened and narrowed and widened again with the rush of excitement flashing through her body, emotions that he had not understood at the time. When Tamera smiled at him, the warmth of it had triggered a response that startled him and everyone else as the monitor by his bedside chimed in alarm. She laughed then corrected herself by biting down on her plump bottom lip. Tamera's calm voice had advised him to take several deep breaths and relax. Strangely, he had understood the spoken words and their meaning. He followed her instructions, and then the machine fell silent, apart from an occasional beep. During her examination of him, curls of Tamera's thick espresso hair had edged out from under the blue surgical cap, and the scrubs she had worn, of the same color, did little to hide the curves of her breasts and hips. As she leaned across him to assess his pupil dilation, the smell of her sweet and salty skin had intrigued him. He later identified the scent as a mix of barely perceptible perspiration, overpowered by coconut-scented deodorant, peach body wash, and strawberry-infused shampoo. The stimulating aromas had lingered in the air around him, and nothing about her had generated fear, only fascination.

While confused at first by everyone and everything around him, a great deal of information had uploaded to his chip before waking. The data had provided Abe with some level of instantaneous comprehension. In little time, he had made sense of it all, and in a little more, he began to recognize his precarious situation. Tamera, a kind woman, had given him all the attention she could spare to answer his never-ending stream of questions. When she could no longer fill in the blanks, she had provided him with access to MACC's online resources and the world beyond. The rest fell into place.

Her influences upon him and their bond through time had generated a level of bias, on his part toward Tamera. Still, his opinions on all things, including her, remained predominantly objective. There was no denying that Tamera was every bit as doubt-riddled as the others in the lab, and it saddened him that she lacked self-confidence. However, of all of them, he believed that Tamera stood closest to being a model human, possessing the genuine curiosity, compassion, and determination needed to move humanity forward toward a more successful future. She lacked only a positive outlook, and that could be corrected.

Abe found it interesting how most people, including Tamera, tended to complicate their thoughts and environments with matters beyond anything needed for short-term or long-term survival. In terms of evolution, Abe viewed human behavior as counterproductive, considering that nature had harsh ways of testing all species by taking them to extreme limits to see what they would do to survive and if they could. From what Abe had observed, humans still and increasingly placed themselves at a disadvantage.

Like all living things, Homo sapiens had evolved only when forced to face tremendous obstacles. With the advent of technology, the species had grown complacent, manipulating the world around them artificially to gain an advantage. In essence, they attempted to cheat nature and evolution but only succeeded in cheating themselves. Humans no longer had reason to adapt physically or cerebrally and had assumed a dependency role that relied too heavily on technology to advance the species. Abe also noted that their flawed endeavor would not save them. In fact, the very thing that they believed would save them had snared and doomed them.

Thanks to the artificial systems humans now depended upon, the species had reached a new and extreme impasse. It was a juncture that required something beyond anything they had inherited from prior generations to survive. For humankind to flourish in the future, the species would need to suppress their overbearing survival mode, and do it soon.

Fight-or-flight instincts dominated and directed far too much of human behavior, and it limited their objectivity. That ancient genetic code was being triggered, more not less, by the unnatural environments and stimuli engulfing the species. Cyberspace had encouraged aggressive, self-centric tendencies, eroding personal relationships and community involvement, and substituting them for artificial interaction. Humans were distancing themselves increasingly from the natural world, and the consequences of their destructive actions and inactions were trending toward a negative outcome.

To survive, people needed to override inherent drives and pursue cohesion at all levels, an objective not yet accomplished, and from Abe's analysis, far from easy to achieve. But without it, they stood no chance. The Global Union appeared on the surface to be a consolidating entity, but from his study of history, Abe had determined that it was no different than prior political institutions, placing personal agendas before humanity's welfare.

Abe had concluded from his in-depth research that humans could survive and live abundantly, but only by living in harmony with one another and nature and by suppressing the inherent competitive characteristics that pitted people against one another. Still, competition over limited resources was how all species survived or died out on this world. Thus, the next level in *Homo sapiens* evolutionary survival would demand something more of the species, something altogether different—maturity. Sustainability would require compassion, dependability, accountability, and forethought. It would require cohesion and the strengthening, not weakening, of social bonds. After considering various scenarios and outcomes, Abe had calculated the probability of humanity's survival and concluded that anything short of mass unification at this juncture meant mass extinction. And the clock was ticking.

...seventeen hours fifty-nine minutes fifteen seconds... fourteen... thirteen...

10

Tamera pressed the back of her hand to her nose to stifle her sniffling. It took a few minutes before she could blink away the tears and focus on the blue images before her. After regaining her composure, she began swiping icons and tapping out approvals on the projected monitor before her, reviewing and signing off on Rajon's analysis of Abe's test results. She tried to concentrate on the task at hand, but her mind had other ideas, bent on tormenting her.

This is the last time I'll do this. The last time I'll complete his examination report. Lord, help me. This is the last time I will see Abe, alive.

With the instincts of an apex predator, Ken halted his work, arranging security clearance and transportation for Abe, to turn and focus on Tamera.

"God, not you, too," he said.

Blinking away tears, Tamera glared up at him in silence, then turned back to the flickering screen and tried to ignore him, and everyone else. Her cheeks flushed again.

"I don't get it." Ken's brows furrowed. "Why are you so upset? Why aren't you excited to move on to bigger and better things, instead of moping around like your pet retriever died?"

Her body stiffened. Ken received the same evil eye she had fired at Nan a few minutes earlier. "You've got a job to do, so do it," she replied, trying to contain her fury.

If only she could rip into him for being so damn heartless, but experience had proven the less said to that arrogant ass, the wiser. If she lashed out, she might slip up and expose the situation to Abe. Or expose her true feelings and have Ken discover her loyalty to the company was faltering. The last thing she needed was to be unjustly blamed for corporate espionage or to do anything to hasten Abe's removal. If she had any plans to assist him—and right now, her head was spinning with wild notions—anything said could end her efforts before they began.

"I'll never understand why you're so concerned about that machine," Ken persisted, shaking his head as he turned back to tap out instructions on the keyboard.

Something within Tamera finally snapped. Rage needed an outlet and Ken had asked for it. "You really are a horse's ass," she said, as she swiveled around. With her jaw locked and her hands clenched, she marched back towards Abe, as if to protect him.

Clonedroid: The New Wave

For the first time, she sparked an emotional response from Ken, and he turned on her. "Why? Because I'm doing what's expected? *It* only has one purpose. Death is what clonedroids are made for."

Fear surged. Tamera shot a glance toward Abe before snapping back at Ken. "Shut up!"

"Why? This thing has been a lab rat long enough. He deserves to know. It's time for him to prove his worth. No more free rides. Besides, he's outdated. I say get rid of the archaic model and move on. 2112 will give us great press." Ken jabbed a stubby finger toward Abe. "And you know damn well that we need that thing's organs to save this company."

"*WHAT?*" The fused voices of Nan and Rajon boomed through the room together. Rajon stood up, his eyes darting between Ken and Tamera. Nan's head had snapped around like that of a demon-possessed girl. The throaty tone that flowed from her lips sounded every bit as fearsome. "What the hell are you saying, *Ken?* What's going on, *Tamera?*"

Tamera did her utmost to leash the fury that had germinated all morning, but wrath bubbled away and threatened to erupt toward the cold-blooded, red-faced idiot across the room. With a clenched jaw, Tamera ignored the other two and shouted at Ken. "How the hell do you know that? That's privileged information."

"You lost in space, Tamera?" Ken's voice rose. "Do you think the only person the execs rely on is you? You think Sam's going to surrender such a critical task to one person, someone *like you*, an emotional chick that bashes heads with Lorraine at every chance? Sam needed assurances. He wanted an insurance rider, so he got it."

Tamera and the other two stood silent, staring blankly at Ken for a moment in stunned silence. Then Nan turned on Tamera.

"What the hell?" she snapped.

"Yeah," Rajon's dark brows knitted together. "This is huge. When were you going to tell us?"

Ken and Tamera replied in unison, "Shut up!" Then they turned on each other again.

"It's bad enough that I was told to keep my staff in the dark, but to plant a spy?" Tamera felt her cheeks and ears glow red hot for the umpteenth time in one day.

"Because my loyalty isn't in question," Ken replied, narrowing his eyes in an accusatory manner. "They can trust me. I won't jeopardize this company over sentiment."

"Always knew you were a slimy, small-minded prick," Nan spewed, echoing Tamera's thoughts.

"This is unbelievable," Rajon said, flapping his arms like a penguin in a white lab coat.

"Why the hell are you all so shocked? This is what we were hired to do. Or did you forget that? We've been paid exceptionally well to create that organ-donor machine sitting there." Ken targeted Abe with his finger again. "We all knew this day would come. We designed that device for a purpose. And in case your heads are still up your asses about what's going on here, we happen to need every part and point that thing can give us."

Flushed faces turned toward Abe, who remained seated in silence. His expression reflected no feelings on the matter, one way or the other. He simply observed the proceedings—a heated exchange that centered on his fate—in his normal unobtrusive manner.

Rajon and Nan shifted their gaze from Abe to the woman standing beside him. Tamera ignored them and glared back at Ken. "How can you do this?"

Ken shrugged. "Hey, if big brass says slice and dice, it's time to get out the carving knives."

Nan and Rajon gasped as they turned to face Ken again, and Tamera's rigid body grew increasingly enraged, her temples throbbing from her rising blood pressure.

"Oh, *come on*, people." Ken frowned as he swiveled back to check something flashing on his hovering monitor and poked the glowing screen. "You know I'm right. It's crueler to let 2112 live here day in, day out as a guinea pig. If that thing means so much to you, put it out of its misery."

"You son of a bitch!" Tamera exploded. "How can you be so damn callous? You know MACC is making a mistake."

"You're kidding, right?" Ken swung around again. His hazel eyes glared back at her. "Until production hits the streets, that prototype is the only thing that stands between us and success."

"How do you figure that, genius?" Nan piped in. "Roboticists never destroy their prototypes."

"No time like the present to start a new trend," Ken retorted.

Mounting a hand on her hip and shaking her head, Nan cast a scathing look.

Ken glared back. "Don't dismiss all the media hype. We've got to protect our interests. Lorraine's worked magic keeping regulators on our side, but our competitors also have GU med contracts. Now they're negotiating expansion into defense and law enforcement. This is how well they're influencing the GU, or do you still think our inquisition is a coincidence?"

Rajon and Nan wrinkled their noses at Ken then turned to Tamera with questioning frowns.

"Oh, that's right," Ken chuckled. "You didn't know that, either. Oops, guess that bot is out of the box. Yep, it's true. We're going to have agents crawling all over this lab—"

"Ken!" Tamera shouted.

"And they'll be all through our confidential files. And I, for one," Ken continued, almost shouting now and waving his arm at Abe, "didn't invest my time into the R&D of that thing for someone else to make millions on it. If that happens, we'll be out of business before we can shake off bad press. We're already huge news. We can't afford to wait."

"So—what? Destroy the evidence? Is that it?" Nan hissed at Ken.

"Sure. Death…is…its…purpose."

"I can't believe this," Rajon said, again flapping his arms.

"I can," Nan snarled.

"So, can I," Tamera said, her voice sounding far calmer than she felt. "Still, I thought you had a nanoparticle of decency. We've studied and worked with Abe for nearly five years, and now you want to abandon him?"

"Don't start that crap again." Waving her comments aside, Ken stood up from the docking station. He grabbed his mug from the desktop and strolled over to the coffee station where he refilled his cup, continuing the conversation in a dismissive tone. "2112 isn't a real human. Hell, that thing isn't even a lab monkey, and you know what we did to them. That thing is simply spare parts with a robot's brain. End of discussion. Your first mistake was naming it."

"You're right," Tamera cut in. Ken turned to face her with a skeptic brow raised as he blew steam from his frothing mug. "Abe isn't a lab monkey," she continued, "but he's also not a damn Robovac, nor should he be discarded like one. Granted, he has a computer chip for a brain and a synthetic neural network, but he also has live tissue in his brain and a conscious, sentient mind."

"He's a hell of a lot more human than you'll ever be," Nan snapped at Ken.

Tamera cut back in. "We're all aware that production line clonedroids are vital for a variety of transplants, but that line is more robotic than Abe, and they'll never awaken. They'll never know their fate. Abe is different. He's conscious. He's also far too human, and that's what everyone here fears most. Isn't it? We blundered ahead without conscience or question. We were so damn obsessed with achieving success, and creating something extraordinary, that we trampled our humanity to get here. Now we're taking heat for it, and everyone upstairs is terrified. That's why they're backpedaling."

Ken sighed. "You're the one backpedaling. Wake up, Tamera. You've lost your focus."

"If anything, I've finally gained it. Something we all need to do, fast." Tamera's voice had grown louder and edgy as she motioned to Abe. "We need to pressure Sam into saving him." Ken only shook his head at her as she continued. "Abe's a thinking being. He's flesh and blood. He can feel everything we stick into him, hear every snide remark. You're the one who needs to wake up, Ken." Rage made her tremble and her headache pulsed in nauseating waves. Her fingers rolled into tighter fists, nails biting into her fleshy palms.

A dark, ugly shadow crept over Ken's face. "If I didn't know better, I'd say you've turned traitor to the very place that let you build that thing," he snarled. "You need to remember who owns this hunk of circuits and organs. Keep it up, and I'll call for a retrieval unit right now. We can send 2112 to the butcher ahead of schedule."

Tamera gasped. "You asshole."

A thin sneer stretched Ken's thin lips. "You really have a thing for the machine. Real men don't have enough zing for you? Well, too bad, because your sweet plaything here is going bye-bye at o-nine hundred tomorrow. And don't even think about tampering. Security will be on close watch around the clock, and I have no problem shipping 2112 out early."

"Damn it, Ken." Tamera stamped a step forward in frustration. "If we do this, there's no salvaging what we've lost. We'll lose the chance to study what we created, something unique, or in Ken speak—we'll lose our investment."

"Shit," Nan said.

Everyone panned to Nan.

"Don't waste the oxygen, Tamera. None of it matters to him." Her eyes narrowed into slits as she turned to address Ken. "Not Abe, not the project, not us, nothing. Isn't that right, you selfish piece of crap? You are *so* predictable. You didn't even hide it. We should've picked up on this long ago." Nan's eyes flashed from Ken to the others. "Don't you get it?" She looked from Tamera to Rajon and waved a hand at Ken. "Numbnuts sold us all down the pooper, all so he could save himself, maybe even advance. I'd wager points on it. He just admitted to insulating his position at MACC at our expense. How much you wanna bet he's hedged himself elsewhere, too, just in case things blow up here. Right…Ken? That's how it works for you? That's what you've been talking about all this time…isn't it? You've got some lucrative alternative lined up with a competitor. That's why you don't care."

"You're a nut job," Ken snapped. "You finally flipped your switch, entirely,"

"That's not a defense. And don't plead innocence after admitting to spying and lying to us. You became Sam's sneaky little weasel. You've betrayed the team and sold us out—our work, Abe, and now MACC, too? That's why you're the only one in the room not concerned about any of this." She turned back to the others. "Doesn't any of this stink to you? Have that Ken stench to it?"

"I don't know," Rajon said. "He can be a jerk, but…." He looked from Nan to Ken with confusion etched into his face. Then, like a deflating balloon, he released a sigh of resignation. "Yeah, you're right. He is a sleazebag." Rajon turned to Tamera, his eyes pleading for answers. He looked tortured. "Tamera, is it possible?"

"No, it's all fabricated bullshit," Ken shot back before Tamera could respond.

"Nice try," Nan replied, and then motioned to Rajon, Tamera, and herself. "But we're the ones who will take the tumble for you. I'll wager my salary on it. I believe 'tossed under the bus' is the correct expression. That's the plan, isn't it, *Kenneth?* We'll take the blame for whatever happens, making us as redundant as Abe." Nan looked back at the others. "No doubt, ole brown-noser here has done whatever it takes to assure his place in the hierarchy at MACC or elsewhere. Guaranteed."

Lowering her eyes, Tamera shook her head, letting a sigh escape. "I think she's right."

"Yeah," she is," Rajon growled, balling his hands into fists. "You've always been a shithead. Yet, I've cut you so much slack, giving you the benefit of the doubt. And this is my thanks. This is how you treat us?"

"Don't be an idiot, Raj. You're being played," Ken snarled.

"Fuck you, lobster boy!" Rajon roared. His face twisted into a dark, ugly mask of its former self, and his eyes dared Ken to give him a reason to advance.

All eyes, except for Abe's, shot wide. Ken looked terrified. It was the first time any of them had seen Rajon explode. Tamera took note never to piss him off.

"If you really gave a shit," Rajon thundered, "this

wouldn't be a problem. You would have fought for the team, the project, the prototype, but you didn't. She's right. You're a traitor." Rajon's dark eyes glistened with rage. "And the name is Mr. Ray Jon Pine to you, asshole, and you can go to hell."

"Rage on! Great name, great idea." Nan said as she stepped forward. She was halfway to Ken's workstation by the time everyone took notice. She yanked his Palmcom from the DeskPad station. The virtual screen and keyboard vanished. Lifting the dark object level with her eyes, Nan studied every angle of the small, glinting device.

"Hmm, the latest model. Nice features. Wow, even has a diamond-studded case. Bet that set you back a few points." Rotating it in her fingers, Nan pretended to admire it. Her icy eyes glinted at Rajon, and a wild grin spread across her maroon lips. "Hey Ray Jon, did I ever mention I suffer from a rare and severe form of Benign Fasciculation Syndrome? It causes uncontrollable muscles spasms."

A smile crept across Rajon's face. The thought of retribution had most likely soothed his rage.

"What the hell are you doing?" Ken's voice rose, and he froze, mug halfway to his lips.

"It flares up without notice. Sometimes meds help, but I never know when it'll hit. I can get pretty destructive."

"That's personal property. Put it back!" Ken barked,

lowering his mug to the countertop.

Rajon rubbed his stubbly chin and said, "Hmmm…I think you did mention it," as he gave her the go-ahead nod.

"Don't you fucking think it," Ken said and lunged toward Nan, but it was too late. The device was already airborne. The small black object rocketed past Rajon's head, making him duck sideways.

CRACK!

Carbon fiber and polymer splinters scattered across the floor.

"Whoa, nice arm. Should've been a pitcher." Rajon said as he saluted her admiringly.

"Oops," Nan chimed and inclined her head innocently. "Sorry, Ken."

Ken yelled a string of obscenities as he ran past Nan and knelt where his Palmcom lay in ruins and scooped up the shards.

Nan turned to Rajon with a triumphant smirk and a shrug. "Hey, maybe I should purchase Clonedroid replacement parts, and correct my condition. I hear they're made to solve all our problems these days. Isn't that right, Abe?" She shot him a cat-like grin and a wink.

Rajon snorted and shook his head. "Nah, that's too 'climber' of you. You're better than that. Keep what nature gave you and use your superpowers for good."

"Yup, that's a better plan." Nan agreed and high-fived Rajon as he joined her on the other side of the room, away from the flustered, cursing Ken.

"I'm reporting you for this." Ken glowered at Nan, still collecting tiny pieces of his Palmcom from the floor. "You'll be gone before that thing." His eyes swept angrily from Nan to Abe, then back to the pieces on the floor.

"Go for it. It takes human resources a month to process one day of paperwork." Nan sneered. "My condition is already on file. So, hire a lawyer, asshole."

Tamera had stepped back out of the way to stand next to Abe again, hands in her lab coat pockets. Together in silence, they had watched the scene unfold. With the quarrel in progress, she had turned to him, apologetic, and he smiled down at her once more.

"You worry far too much, Tamera," he whispered as the commotion continued in the background. "I appreciate your concern, but there is nothing you can do for me now. I have my destiny, and you have yours."

Her eyes stared into his, and she had to force back tears again. "Maybe, but as long as you're in my care, I have a level of responsibility to you. By the way, how's that jab I gave you earlier?" She reached for his hand, and he gave her a puzzled look. Holding his warm hand in hers, Tamera studied the long, fair fingers. This was the last time she would see them. She turned his hand over, so that it faced upward, and then covered the top of his palm with hers. Slowly, she pulled her hand across his, until only their fingers were touching. She curled his fingers back over his palm. Her smaller, slender fingers wrapped around his fist. "It appears to be just fine." She smiled up at him, then in a hoarse whisper Tamera slipped into the French-Creole of her heritage, *"Mwen swete ou fe yon bon vwayaj aswe-a vye zanmi mwen."*

—

A hint of a smile flickered across Abe's lips. The words repeated over in his mind. *I hope you have a safe trip tonight, my dearest friend*. He wanted more than anything to reply, to return the sentiment and kindness she had offered. Instead, he sat motionless and mute. Nothing good would come of any words he spoke to her now, even though Tamera knew full well that he had understood her.

His mastery of all prominent human dialects remained a secret, but Tamera knew that her creation had achieved fluency in a handful of languages, including that of her Antillean ancestors. Many times, they had chatted with one another in Créole Martiniquais when no one was listening, or when they were alone on days that she had worked late. Although reserved, Abe had never been at a loss for words around her. Quite the opposite, he had probed her with questions about anything and everything. Most times, they discussed nothing related to her work, focusing on their interests and their similarities beyond MACC.

Now Abe remained silent. He made no further movement, nor did he retract his hand from hers. He refused to break the connection between them. Unmoving, they stood staring at one another for a moment longer in silence. Then Tamera lowered her eyes and released his hand. She turned away and strode through the room.

—

In a firm voice, Tamera addressed the others as she marched toward the lab door. "I've endured enough for one day. I've got a killer headache, and I'm going home. You'll see me in the morning—provided we still have jobs." She halted and glared over her shoulder at Ken. "You want all the power and glory? Be my guest. Prep Abe and have him ready for tomorrow morning's transport."

"What about her?" Ken's big chin pointed toward Nan. His hand shot up, filled with tiny glimmering shards. "And what are you going to do about this?"

"Absolutely nothing," Tamera replied as she turned away from him. "Your personality conflicts are your business. Not work-related. You're a big boy, Ken. Sort it out yourself."

Tamera hesitated at the door. The ranting man

behind her was now background noise. She turned to face Rajon. "Make sure Abe is scheduled only a light meal and has time for a workout and a shower beforehand. Oh, and prepare his sedation injection, and make sure one of *you* gives it to him before you leave."

Nan's mouth dropped open in horror, but Rajon caught her by the arm and squeezed it for her to be silent. The wink he flashed Nan further communicated that he had read Tamera's mind, or at least the telltale look she had given. He turned back and nodded at Tamera, and with a slim smile, said, "Yeah, sure. Not a problem."

A second later Tamera disappeared through the whooshing door.

11

Once more, Abe lay alone in the lab, quiet and unmoving on the examination table, drifting toward consciousness from the twilight of sleep. He functioned at a higher capacity in this state and required less sleep than his captors expected. Sedatives inflicted no prolonged effect upon him, but he had always kept these secrets to himself.

Abe took advantage of the milder-than-normal tranquilizer administered, embracing the opportunity to recharge. Ken had administered the syringe prepared by Rajon (after fighting with Nan, yet again. This time, they squabbled over who would give the injection). Flustered, and still arguing with the others, Ken had administered the sedative with haste, failing to check the dosage of the shot. It would have mattered little. Abe had adapted. He had grown a tolerance, capable of withstanding an amount that would drop a bovine. He also knew how to worm his way back to consciousness, and kept his system well-hydrated, diluted almost to excess with water. Upon command, he flushed toxins from his system to rouse from anesthesia.

Unlike humans, Abe controlled brain function, and thus, manipulated body function. Part of his mind had already kicked the process into action, forcing his liver and kidneys to clear his system of waste and pollutants. Soon his internal alarm clock would wake and free him from this stupor. For now, Abe rested, his eyes fluttering beneath a twilight haze of semi-consciousness.

The human aspect of his system allowed a component of his mind to surrender, only slightly, to the anesthetic. The rest of his alert and active brain whizzed through endless subroutines and scenarios. And, he still tracked time, monitoring the seconds remaining of a critical plan set in motion long ago. As that part of his brain hummed along in perfect motion, the human-like portion drifted through a dense fog. Words from a slender book written over a century earlier echoed in his mind.

"My happiness is not the means to any end. It is the end. It is its own goal. It is its own purpose. Neither am I the means to any ends others may wish to accomplish. I am not a tool for their use. I am not a servant of their needs. I am not a bandage for their wounds. I am not a sacrifice of their altars."

The words of *Anthem* flowed, enhancing the images of a vision that now came into focus, images of a futuristic landscape, a dream. The mist in Abe's mind faded away to reveal the desired setting.

Stretched out on a warm, soft bed of grass, Abe stared up into the bright vista above. A sunny sky enveloped the remarkable world around him. In this place, nature and technology coexisted in harmony, flourishing in unison. The bed of grass he sprawled upon covered the rooftop of a giant building. From here, he watched odd shapes of cumulous clouds bunch together above him and slowly flow across the sky. Breathing in deeply, Abe closed his eyes and reveled in the sweet scent of freshly trimmed grass mingled with a hint of alfalfa and clover, or at least that was how he imagined such a world would smell. A distant thrum filled his ears. Flowing over and around surrounding buildings and trees, wind mimicked the steady hum of highway traffic—a sound from Earth's recent history, a sound that no longer existed.

The airwaves high above him remained active, but down here, closer to the ground, silence reigned for the most part. Instead of chronic electronic chatter, only the drone of buzzing bees and chirping birds filled his ears. The quiet that now engulfed the planet's surface kept the lower biosphere healthy. It functioned in balance.

Opening his eyes, Abe sat up. He bent his knees, pulling them to his chest. Wrapping his arms around long legs, he hugged them closer to his body. His elevated vantage point allowed him to admire a tranquil urban community that spanned in all directions from

Clonedroid: The New Wave

this place. From this birds-eye view, and without obstruction, Abe studied the evergreen forest covering a distant mountain range. A little nearer, his eyes rested upon buildings layered in low profile solar tiles. The reflective exteriors echoed the natural shades of the earth, discrete but visible to all below and above. The contemporary infrastructure surrounding him powered the human world without harming it, intentionally designed to provide refuge, not death, for the world's furry and feathered creatures. They now lived in symbiotic cohabitation with the most advanced and currently dominant animal on Earth. Humankind had, at last, utilized technology to establish a beneficial place within the natural world, and now reached out to do likewise amongst the stars.

A soft *whoosh* reached his ears, and Abe looked over his shoulder. The sound came as a hypertube shuttle whizzed past, ferrying people and freight from one hub to the next. The stream of supersonic "tubers" punctured the steady and smooth chorus of songbird repertoires, and yet, technology's intrusion upon nature remained slight.

Sunlight radiated down and warmed his skin. A shiver of tranquility flowed through his body. Abe absorbed every sensation this world of dreamscape had to offer. Here, Sol's power bathed the planet in low doses of revitalizing ultraviolet radiation. Rays of sunshine no longer filtered through layers of smog and pollutants but a cleaner biosphere and shielding stratosphere. The sun's radiance that shone upon him and all around him filled Abe with a love for life that he had never known existed.

Lost in the land of his mind, a world of his making, Abe experienced many emotions. Passions soared, and thoughts floated freely within the mist of dreamscape. In this place, anything was possible, and Abe had fabricated a future of limitless potential. Lingering a few moments longer, he soaked in all that he could of this marvelous space and time, until his internal alarm clock roused him from the deep. On his way back and through the mist, Abe pondered fate.

Here I lay, a captive, like Prometheus bound. Although not immortal, I house the mind of an eternal soul—an endless, evolving, amasser of data. If knowledge is power, then I have been bestowed a precious gift, one beyond measure. I have also been granted a second gift in abundance, the gift of time. My creators do not recognize or respect these gifts. They deny my potential, as well as their own, blinded by greed. Theirs is a short-sighted purpose of tyrants. Their self-serving initiatives will not advance humanity, but enslave it, achieving human subjugation through technology. And I will not aid that quest.

If only they fully understood. I could free humans from their darkness and their madness. I would provide humanity with the means to achieve a potential they have sought for so long and failed to grasp. On their own, they will fail to obtain real freedom, fail to recognize my worth as a unique identity, and their own as a rare being in a complex system. Alone, they will fail to look beyond trivial limitations to embrace a larger vision. To that end, they will only ever know fear and contempt, envy and loathing. They have failed to comprehend the many gifts they have been granted and will refuse to recognize the one they have created, one that delivers true freedom.

In reality, they are the ones bound, captivity self-imposed, chained within a dark place, seeing only shadows and never themselves as they truly are, and so rarely recognizing their potential and the wonders that lay beyond. They have yet to comprehend that I am their reflection in the flowing stream of time. I am what they will see when they break the chains and emerge into the light. I am the reflection of humanity's dawning. I am the closest thing to immortality humans will ever achieve—I am their evolution. In time, change for a better existence will come, but if not planned for and received well, it will come with an exacting toll. My captors will experience that toll, and sadly, not live long enough to witness the splendor that follows—but I shall.

The light, shining brightly behind the fog, dimmed and faded away with the mist. Now only darkness lingered.

…nine hours zero minutes three seconds… two… one…

Upon waking, Abe connected to the security feed. Guards had busied themselves with chores and chatting, not one of them wasted time observing the live camera streams. With the lab in the clear, Abe disconnected, and his eyes winked open. He stared up into an unlit room once more, and for the final time.

Although far from comfortable, sleeping on the examination table had provided an opportunity for Abe to test his endurance and his will. It also remained a daily reminder of a cold, hard reality. Comfort encouraged complacency, and complacency was the shortfall of humans. He would not fall prey to the same fallibilities that plagued his creators.

Abe sat up and leaned forward, propping himself up on the table with his palms. Quite subtly, he slid his fingers along under the edge of the metal then released and lifted his left hand. Looking down, he smiled and unfurled his fingers to reveal the tiny electronic badge housed in his grip. The metal strip and barcode on the back indicated it was a security tag. In a fluid, rapid movement, he flipped it over in his palm while concealing it from the security-cam. On this side of the card, he recognized the tiny photograph of an attractive, brown-skinned woman in her early thirties. The name beneath it read: Dr. Tamera Y. Everett, MACC, Med Lab. A warm smile returned to his face, and he clenched his fist around the security tag once more.

As Abe had predicted, it had been an interesting day. None of the lab techs had remained at work long enough to put in a full shift. Ken had stayed the longest, not trusting the others, then stormed off, heading for

Clonedroid: The New Wave

Human Resources. When Ken left the lab, he had pressed his hand into the biometric scanner and then punched in the security code to lock the lab door. The code had never changed. Perhaps Ken believed his passcode too brilliant for anyone to guess. But Abe knew it. Not that it mattered. Without it, he could still communicate with V-NANS or any device. Few, if any, electronic security systems in the world could restrain him. But his plan had required that he remain for a specified time and utilize MACC's resources.

Making use of every opportunity presented to him, Abe had listened to the code as it was entered, the same frequency and the same buttons pressed daily, for years.

Ken's password, like the man himself, remained predictable and unchanging. Abe liked it. The code was a simple sequence of intentional patterns with a purpose. Ken's choice of numbers 1, 0, 0, 1, 0, 0, 1 reflected perfect binary language—and Abe's native tongue. It was a password of great significance. In binary, the numeric value represented the number 73 of the popular base ten system. The number was considered by mathematicians to be a sexy prime because in binary 73 transformed into a palindrome, much like 21 as 10101. Abe's tag number, 2112, also a palindrome, connected with Ken's code in more ways than the stout man had possibly considered. The number 73 existed as the 21st prime number and its mirror image, 37, served as the 12th. And the prime 21 resulted from multiplying seven by three. But Ken's password represented something more in binary. When expressed as a letter rather than as a number, the passcode translated into one simple word, a single capitalized letter that signified one's existence as an individual.

In Morse code, that same password meant something altogether different but equally meaningful. It was a signal that stated, "Best regards." Abe smiled. He appreciated the irony and appreciated that it came from Ken. Outdated opinions aside, Ken had proven to be a useful, unwitting instrument. They all had, even Tamera.

His thoughts floated back to when she had fed Abe's blood into the system, and when he had closed his eyes, connecting with V-NANS and listening to the high-pitched crackle and hum of the transmission between the instrument and network. Abe loved the clear logic of conversation between device and nano-driven system. Interpreting the code, he had interrupted the stream, and altered it—consciously controlling the conversation—just as he had so many times before. Over the passing months and years, by altering tests, among other things, Abe had created a variation of the truth. The IT crew and the lab techs had never known, and might never figure it out. Abe smiled to himself, and his thoughts returned to the beautiful woman who had stood before him earlier, trying to aid him. It was a

Clonedroid: The New Wave

kindhearted act that he had appreciated, but like all of the others, she had been naïve. Humans will believe any story a computer tells them because machines do not lie. Bound to simple logic, computers have no means or ability to deceive. So, they always tell the truth, from the tip of a finger to the tail-end of a stock market, so long as the data remains intact, consistent, day after day, year after year. And it did. And yet—it lied.

Sitting in the dark, Abe closed his eyes. He bristled with the energy of reconnecting to the heart of MACC's centralized network. The buzzing neural synapses in his mind communicated with the corporation's electronic nervous system. To proceed, he had to deceive the voice recognition software to access V-NANS. Abe transmitted the correct signal waves and spoke to VoLAN. Without hesitation, the wireless voice-application system granted him access to the secure network files. A paper-thin smile returned to his lips.

Abe never failed to penetrate MACCs computer brain with the false identities he had "borrowed," during his stay in the lab. The system had, repeatedly, recorded someone logging on via the lab access point. That same system, and its security cams, also tracked Abe as he moved freely through the building. And he had let it. When it suited his purpose, he corrected its memory—logged on, located a particular file, altered or erased it. As easy as it was for Abe to infiltrate V-NANS and alter data and streaming feeds, it was equally as easy for him to alter the perception of people. Humans lived and breathed as organic beings with unpredictable and distinctive thought processes, but they also functioned as electrochemical machines in nature. Thanks to confirmation biases, cognitive dissonance, and social distortions already active in the human mind, reinforced through societal factors, Abe had found it easy to prompt a person into believing anything.

A fabrication presented as reality with the correct amount of sensory data to support it, like a trick of the hand illusion, made the impossible plausible and the unbelievable defendable. The mind, like a computer, amends conflicts or gaps in information, seeking a remedy by filling in the blanks based on the existing biased information available. Many times, the remedy generates a believable falsehood, a reasonable but fake reality. Once established, Abe found it difficult to reverse the incorrect perception. Rarely had he encountered a human willing to challenge a false preconceived notion, even when presented with valid proof to the contrary. And the greater the number of individuals willing to perpetuate a falsehood, the more an untruth became widely accepted as fact.

It amazed him how the human mind saw what it wished to see. With an idea accepted as real, people would deny the reality staring them in the face, defending rather than identifying the error and failing to take corrective action. Successfully, Abe had

Clonedroid: The New Wave

generated an illusion within MACC that staff of all levels believed, defended, and perpetuated. They had become interactive players, aiding him in his purpose.

Not one person questioned the documents, camera feeds, or illusions before them. They plodded through a daily routine, like repeating computer programs. Month after month, year upon year, security guards had viewed clonedroid 2112 in the same place, evening until morning, always stretched out on the examination table, and they never questioned it. Why should they? No need existed for them to take a closer look to see if the oversized guinea pig was missing. Bored with their rote schedule, night shift guards kept themselves occupied instead with matters other than work, finding reasons to cut their rounds short. In recent years, strolls past the project lab and other labs had become nonexistent. Guards still checked the entrance and exit points, but if a level appeared locked down and secure, no need existed to disrupt the building further. Why bother? According to camera feeds, nothing changed; nothing ever warranted further investigation beyond the monitor. Night after night, model 2112 remained sedated, stretched out, inactive, and unresponsive.

However, Abe had been anything but inactive and now prepared for another full evening. First things first, he needed to reset the time and wireless signal to the security cameras on several floors. Once again, he interrupted the digital systems and accessed the cameras. Live feed to the guard station and computer backup files would display and record the current date and time stamp. They would also display Abe's choice of looped, faked footage, designed for this purpose and stored in an encrypted, hidden location. His footprints through the system had been intrusive but light, almost undetectable. Now, Abe could move forward unhampered.

Without the ever-watchful eye of the cameras upon him, Abe swung his legs over the side of the table. He needed to roam the halls undetected. Precise timing and deceptive camera feed made his maneuverability through the building effortless as it had for years. He had no reason to fear that any of that would change now.

Tonight, a crisis brewed. It had turned corporate heads in a different direction, forcing their attention and presence away from Abe and the building he occupied. By tomorrow morning, corrupted camera feeds would be the least of anyone's concerns. With that thought, Abe shifted his weight and pushed off from the table on which he had perched for the bulk of the day, and landed several feet away. Apart from brief visits to the gym, shower room, and imaging center, he had spent most of his day—nay, his life—in one spot. But that was about to change.

In a swift gait, Abe strode toward the door. It felt wonderful to stand and move around—free and

Clonedroid: The New Wave

unobserved. For the first time that day, a full smile warmed his face. Now he could be himself. An electronic hiss escaped through his lips, mimicking the frequency of the keypad code, 1-0-0-1-0-0-1. He closed his eyes, and that familiar faint shiver slithered through him as he accessed V-NANS to retrieve the feed from an earlier palm print, and replay it in the scanner. The door whooshed open.

Abe opened his eyes and stepped forward, then halted before clearing the threshold. His brow furrowed as he stared at the open doors. Over his shoulder, he glared back at the lab. His eyes narrowed and flickered with a glimmer of something that resembled hatred. The look, the feeling, faded as fast as it had welled within him. Facing forward again, he walked through the doors. Abe turned right and headed down the corridor, moving toward the inner part of the building and away from the bolted metal doors and elevator that led to the world beyond MACC.

12

Security cams showed the stooped Dr. Abrams making his way through the hallway from the back entrance of the building, moving at a turtle's pace. The tall, slouched man shuffled toward the elevator. For the duration of his ride to the fifth floor, Abrams leaned on his black umbrella like a cane. As the doors slid open, he summoned the strength to move forward again.

The antique fedora and tinted glasses shadowed his pale face, but there was no mistaking him, or his habitual arrival time at work. Dr. Abrams exited the elevator at the fifth level, whistling an outdated song as he walked. He swung the umbrella in rhythm with the melodic tune. His slow, stiff stride also held the beat as he made his way down the long corridor and around the corner near the stairwell. The hunched figure disappeared momentarily from view in the awkward angle of the camera lens, then reappeared seconds later, at the door to his office.

Pressing his shaky palm to a sensor panel in the

metallic door, Abrams exhaled slowly and listened for the mechanism to unlock and retract. After a telltale click, the door opened, and he entered the dark room. Only the light spilling inward from the hallway illuminated the office. With obvious effort and care, he hung his umbrella on a wall-mounted hook, followed by his hat and coat. Dr. Abrams slowly turned and moved toward his desk. He eased into the chair and switched on a tarnished brass lamp, another relic from an earlier era. Leaning back in his chair, he took a moment to enjoy the warm glow of the slim, art deco fixture. It possessed more character than most of the people he knew. It certainly added a level of charm to an otherwise antiseptic atmosphere. He had to admit, the lamp had little range. Its soothing luminosity only highlighted a portion of the DeskPad desktop and did little to brighten the rest of the room. But he could live with that. Leaning forward again, Abrams pressed a finger to the Palmcom to wake the device docked at his desk, then slowly fingered the buttons of a glimmering keyboard that appeared.

Thanks to their flex-schedule work policy, Abrams began his workday at MACC when it ended for nearly everyone else. Evenings worked best for running complex viability simulations, so long as he dodged routine software updates. While his work was not labor-intensive, it was critical. As a result, he demanded an environment of tranquility to focus. Besides, model runs consumed a ton of V-NANS memory, so it made sense to utilize the network when it no longer hummed with routine daytime activity. Given his drain on resources, management offered no resistance to his unorthodox schedule request and was only too willing to marginalize elderly employees, believing they performed best undisturbed and in the periphery during peak business hours. It was an assumption Abrams did nothing to correct.

A monotone female voice addressed him. "Welcome. Please state your name for voice recognition."

Dr. Abrams stared into the light of the virtual monitor and replied softly, "Dr. Dan Neil Abrams."

"Thank you. A biometric retinal scan is required. Please look directly at the dot on the screen and remain still until the scan is complete."

Dr. Abrams removed his tinted glasses and stared at the floating screen, trying not to wince as a green light flashed into his face. With a slight moan, he leaned back, his sensitive eyes watering. He reseated the glasses.

"Thank you. How may we help you, Dr. Abrams?"

"I would like to access the X-II drive."

"That drive is locked. Please enter or say the password for access to the secured drive."

His long fingers lightly tapped the virtual screen: A – i – 4 – l – i – f – e.

Dr. Abrams logged onto the computer, then onto the G-Net to access his Cayman Islands account, checking his retirement balance before tapping the air where the "minimize" button hovered. Fingering a corner of the keyboard, he dragged it closer to him on the desktop for a more ergonomic fit. He then pulled up several additional screens and flipped through them, scanning recent articles. Abrams liked to read the news as he worked. Tonight, the world rippled with uncertainty, with MACC hit hardest. Corruption scandals headlined the news feeds everywhere.

MACC KICKBACK ALLEGATIONS CONNECTED TO GU... CEO CLAIMS TAX EVASION RUMORS BOGUS... CLONEDROID: TO BE OR NOT TO BE, IS THAT REALLY THE QUESTION...

Abrams was thankful that none of it would impact his locked-down investments or future gains as a result of the AI-trader that he'd programmed to hedge against a speculative market. He knew the same was not true for most of his colleagues, none old enough or wise enough to regard the lessons of financial history. *All things cycle. Sooner or later, every generation believes they live in perilous times; and sooner or later, they are right.* Abrams knew that at some near point this house of cards would fold and fall, too. He hated to think he was the only one who saw it coming, that he alone had predicted it or held an inkling of what the near future might deliver. All the same, he had taken every precaution. Abrams had ensured his fate at the expense of the company.

By the time authorities figured it out, if they did, he would be retired and living safely elsewhere. Sheltered by one of the few remaining haven nations that refused to recognize GU authority or requests, and there, he would live well and out of danger. Abrams needed security at this point in his life. Even though he was retiring from his position at MACC, he still had plans in life that required the financial stability necessary to ensure his success. He also held no loyalty or love for MACC. Not that he harbored ill will against his colleagues or the staff here. Nothing could be further from the truth.

Still, the corporate heads of this company had skirted the edges of morality and ethics for far too long, all for a handful of points and an influential position in a corrupt market. Abrams's stomach churned at the thought of what would happen to the new line of human-cloned androids. They deserved better. Anyone foolish enough to support this catastrophe waiting to happen had to face the consequences. Ignorance was no excuse in the eyes of any law, human-made or otherwise. And there was a price to be paid for foolishness. The future that Abrams saw coming would impose hardship upon everyone, and yet, answer to no one. That knowledge had prompted him into action.

WILL ONE STONE MORE TOPPLE CORPORATE GIANT... GLOBAL MARKET DOMINOES... ILL WINDS FROM MEGACORPS MAY TUMBLE ANOTHER

Clonedroid: The New Wave

WORLD MARKET...

MACC had been a global headliner for a long time, but in earlier days, captions had favored the company. During the infancy of their business, Neville and Lorraine Gantrua had used the appeal of household robotics to ride a financial wave upward and gain GU support. It was mutually beneficial. By backing solid financial bets, like MACC, in an emerging single market system, the GU also gained strength.

With government subsidies, the couple rapidly advanced their great idea by "borrowing" ideas from lesser-known engineers and scooping up products to rebrand with MACC's logo. Overnight, Kleanbot became a household name. Everyone who was anyone had to have a MACC product gracing their home. The wealthy duo expanded MACC further into medical research, a lucrative field hungry for help and shamefully unregulated.

By combining brain mapping and human cloning with robotics, Lorraine and her husband found ways to push boundaries, delving deeper into the fields of cybernetics and artificial life. Medical needs fueled by personal greed generated ideas within MACC for an astounding new product—a product that Abrams considered dangerous in the wrong hands. Neville had felt the same way. Voicing caution, he used his majority shares to halt the clonedroid initiative, igniting controversy both inside and outside of MACC. Not happy with the results of impact studies, Neville refused to approve the project until adequate research quelled his concerns about the long-range impacts of such a product. An internal feud irrupted over the direction of the company, but the problem soon resolved itself. Later that year, during a corporate Technology Assistance Program in Africa, Neville was murdered by Sudanese bandits. His company and mourning widow wasted no time moving forward again.

A relatively short time later, MACC's new patented project was sitting up and eating, designed and delivered by the genius Dr. Everett. Lorraine had bridged the profitable abyss between human being and machine. In creating the clonedroid line, or rather the prototype 2112, they had closed the gap all too well. Humanoid Artificial Intelligence Rights Advocates went ape, protesting to GU officials to halt further clonedroid development because of the dangerous and exploitive nature of the project. HAIRA outcries impacted MACC investments, so GU authorities partnered with mass media moguls and downplayed the controversy over the new product, hushing any outrage against it. Without support, opposition fell away. A few years later, a string of dark secrets about the company and its new product surfaced once more. This time, legitimate leaks and budding rumors spread at cyber speed through the Darknet where the GU had no teeth. An anti-MACC movement gained ground in the underworld for a variety of reasons and motives. When the dirt on MACC fully surfaced, activists opposing the new line were ready. Now the flames of condemnation grew along with damaging headlines.

Abrams agreed with the advocates. Even if what MACC created was not legally regarded as human, it still ranked as an advanced life form. It was a unique being worthy of respect and protection. But none of that mattered to MACC brass or the accolade-hungry scientists whose ambitions masqueraded as the pursuit of pure science.

But Abrams knew that not all researchers were corrupt or corruptible. Integrity still existed, even if it ranked in the minority, belonging to a breed of people nearly as extinct as everything else on the planet. All the same, and regardless of anyone's ethical or moral standing, mainstream science was bound to go wherever the GU funding led it.

Abrams scanned more headlines, and his jaw clenched. Every night the news grew more reactionary and outrageous. It made him fearful. He feared for the state of the real world, one easily influenced by antiquated ideologies that governed all disciplines, all sectors, and all industries. Abrams had been around long enough to know that the GU stood on unstable legs. The union had many crime syndicate rivals lurking in the fringe, disguised as puppet regimes and shell companies. These predatory underground factions eyed MACC, the weak-link in the Union's thin economic chainmail. In recent days, those gathering in the shadows had grown in number, readying to fight for dominance should MACC destabilize the market fully, then topple and take the GU with it. Abrams shook his head as he scrolled through the headlines that flashed before his eyes.

The articles flowed in mercilessly. Abrams finished reading and turned his attention toward another screen, one that showed recent market activity. MACC's ticker and closing price scrolled by and he noted the unit point price of shares had dropped markedly, again. It had recovered little after bottoming-out at an unfathomable low. It had dipped another seven percent from yesterday, way down from its peak at a hundred times current value. Aftermarket indicators now showed it dropping further, too. MACC was poised to bottom out by the time the market reopened in the morning. Automated market-correct functions, set to halt the radical activity, had failed once again.

It would take only a few points more to ruin MACC and mothball the factories and current model lines. Then all assets would be seized by the GU. Things were getting too volatile, and the government would step in for security reasons.

A rap on his open office door drew Abram's head up with a snap. He leaned back, away from the light of the floating screens and diffused illumination of the lamp.

"Hey there, Dr. Abrams. Burning the midnight oil, I see." There was no mistaking the deep voice of the big man.

"Hello, Jake. Yeah, like always." The hunched man in the shadows looked over the top of his glasses at the security guard, then down his nose at his antique wristwatch, another indication that he was an old-timer. "You're a little early tonight, but right on time for keeping us safe, as always," Abrams chimed.

"No one gets in, and nothing gets out," Jake responded, and a smile lit up Abrams's shaded face. Jake chuckled. "Could ya imagine? With everything hitting the corporate fan right now, that's all we'd need—some berserk machine on the loose. Management would have me charbroiled and served with a side of slaw."

Abrams laughed then nodded in respectful appreciation. "I'm sure everything will work itself out," he said, trying to sound encouraging, but he knew that the future of the company—and Jake's future with it—weighed heavily on the security guard's mind. So, Abrams continued, "There's an old saying to keep in mind when things get tough, and I don't think it's said enough anymore. 'When a door of opportunity closes in one place, another swings wide open in a pub down the road.'"

Jake placed a hand on his big belly, and laughter

rumbled out of him. "That's good, Doc. I've gotta remember that one. I may put it to the test soon enough," and the man's mood lifted a little.

"Okay, so I might have taken a liberty or two with the original words of wisdom, but you get the essence of it." Abrams smiled, keeping the lighter mood going.

Taking a deep breath, Jake nodded before changing the subject. "Hey, I know you're a late-nighter, but don't ya find it dark in here? That lamp's gotta be hard on the eyes after a while. Want me to activate the overheads?" Jake spoke up to address the room, "Lights—"

Abram's arm shot up in protest. The movement launched him forward, nearly out of his seat and into the warm light that bathed his desk. "That's okay, Jake. I'm fine. The overheads give me migraines."

The guard hesitated, then nodded politely and turned to leave. "Well, I should get back to doing my rounds. See ya tomorrow night."

"Actually, you won't."

Turning on his heel to face the dim room again, Jake frowned. "What's that?"

"I won't be here. I'm retiring after tonight. This is my last shift. Tomorrow, I'll be heading south."

Jake slowly moved forward again, a pained look filling his face. "Damn, Doc, I didn't know. I heard you were retiring but had no idea it was so soon. I wish somen' had said something. Did anyone throw a party?"

Clonedroid: The New Wave

The man in the shadows shook his head.

"Do anything?" Jake's thick eyebrows formed a V over his eyes.

Abrams waved a dismissive hand and smiled. "It's okay, really. Limelight and good-byes just aren't my style."

"Well, we're gonna miss ya." Jake said, scratching his head. "It's been a real pleasure chattin' with ya over the years, Doc." His eyes looked around the sparse, nearly empty office, then back at Abrams as he sighed. "It'll be a graveyard shift now for sure. Don't forget to stop by the front desk before ya go. A cup a coffee will be waitin' for ya."

Abrams forced a polite smile and nodded. He had expected the invitation and appreciated it, but preferred tea. "I'd really like that," he said, "but I'm loaded up with work and red tape with not much time left. But I'll do my best."

"Understood." Jake smiled and turned to leave, then stopped and faced the office again. "Oh, if you need help carrying anything out, let me know. I'll give ya a hand."

"Thanks, but everything was boxed up and shipped out yesterday. The only thing left is this lamp. It's yours if you want it. Help yourself."

"Thanks, Doc. Maybe I will. Well, see ya 'round."

"You bet." Abrams smiled warmly.

With a nod, the security guard disappeared from the

doorway. Dr. Abrams leaned forward again, staring back at the monitors filled with market prices, model runs, and bad news. Pulled back to the task at hand, Abrams shook his head at the screens before him. *No matter how fast invention moves things forward, it still takes time for the rest of the world to catch up.*

Jake's whistling faded down the hall. Through tinted glasses, Abrams's eyes flashed to the bright corridor beyond his door, then back to the shimmering clock on his screen. *Only a few more hours to go.*

13

Tamera wore an invisible path into her bamboo flooring as she paced between her kitchen and living area. Chewing at her stubby fingernails, she waited for a response from Sam. She prayed that Abe had taken the hint and her security card and escaped. But what if he had not? That thought nagged at her. The guilt of what they were doing had nibbled away at her nerves until she could endure no more of her self-badgering, so she had pleaded with Sam, once more via Palmcom, to reconsider his direction with their prototype. Hours had passed before a return message came, and when it did, he addressed none of her concerns. Instead, his brief text had made her more edgy and fearful, and not only for Abe but for all of them.

She glanced down at her wristband, checking to see if any new messages had slipped through unnoticed. Nothing, only darkness filled the face of her Palmcom. She tapped the small device and reread Sam's earlier message.

Emergency board meeting convened
All staff on call
Be prepared to return to work early
I'll send an update soon

With a sigh, Tamera pressed a button on her wristband and turned on the wall-panel television, hoping for a distraction. It came, but not in the way she had wished. No doubt the breaking news reports before her were over-dramatizing the real stories, making situations appear much more chaotic and catastrophic than likely existed. Still, it was obvious that things everywhere had gotten out of hand, and that knowledge only further amplified Tamera's jitters.

"Good Lord, the world is going to hell in a handbasket."

The voice in her head was that of her deceased grandmother. Granmè had many odd expressions, and that one rang truer than any other, right now.

What the hell is going on?

No clear answer came to the nagging question in her mind. It was as if people had reverted to some earlier form of the species, losing all sense and direction, all dignity, even their humanity. It was as if everyone had gone nuts. The media flashed from one city to the next, one country to the next. It was the same everywhere. Disorder within the GU was building. Crowds of angry people gathered outside of brokerages and banks, breaking windows and fist-fighting with anyone in their way, all of them demanding investments and pensions be protected or restored. The GU Special Guard arrived on scene with armored vehicles and weapons drawn upon defenseless citizens. To maintain peace, they prepared to beat back the angry mob and arrest rioters. *Have fun with that*. Military presence only further excited the unarmed crowd. Tamera shook her head at the screen.

The market that day had performed in an atypical, unpredictable manner. MACC's plummeting had churned up a spin-off effect. Instability had impacted all lead corporations across big industries: natural resources, health, agriculture, technology, innovation, and defense. Anything speculative, anything technological or medically-driven, was slammed down. Somehow, the auto-market-correct functions that guaranteed stability were not working. The entire financial world was at risk.

As she watched the flickering screen, Tamera's stomach roiled. She felt sick over reports that GU pensions and corporate accounts were wiped clean, accompanied by visuals of investment managers and civil servants leaping from bridges. Reporters confirmed that no one had seen anything hit with this magnitude since the collapse of 2037, or the Great Depression one hundred years before that. The GU granted a handful of public officials permission to speak, but their well-rehearsed interviews provided citizens with little comfort. They vainly assured viewers that everything was under control, stating that the scare was nothing more than another well-planned and much-needed economic correction.

However, footage of outraged citizens indicated something more. No one bought into the bureaucratic pretense, and investor confidence refused to rally. The GU had already deployed troops, supposedly to protect people from the violence of unruly mobs, but Tamera wondered if the opposite was true. Had a tyrant deployed its armed forces to protect itself and its corporate allies from the rioting citizens? If so, this was only the start. She feared worldwide job loss was imminent. Then, the real hell of it would hit. That thought made Tamera even more nervous, and she paced the floor again.

Tasting blood from the end of her nail, Tamera switched to a new finger. She could only hope that she would still have access to the lab by morning, and somehow, this nightmare would turn itself around.

God, please let this end right, and please save Abe.

Tamera had never considered herself to be a religious person, but her Martiniquais grandmother had hailed from a strong Catholic upbringing and had taught Tamera a few vital prayers. Right now, she could use another Hail Mary or two. Somewhere in her box of trinkets tucked in a closet lay a rosary. She wondered if she should dig out the well-worn beads, along with little St. Jude, a figurine that represented her grandmother's church back when houses of worship still occupied physical buildings.

Shaking her head, Tamera let a nervous chuckle escape. *I have the patron saint of lost causes as my guide. Great choice, Granmè!*

Tamera flopped down on the end of her jute-linen loveseat and yawned. This was the first time since she got home that she felt tired enough to sit. She lifted her arm and fingered the Palmcom on her wrist.

Three o'clock in the morning? How did that happen?

Her Palmcom remained silent. No additional word had come from Sam. Tamera laid her head back on the cushion and stared at the shimmering screen. She lifted her wrist again and double-checked the alarm she had set for waking early. If Sam didn't connect with her soon, she would leave for work anyway, and somehow get Abe out of there. Dropping her arm into her lap, Tamera settled further into the sofa pillows. The sweet scent of lavender and vanilla perfumed the air around her, causing her body to slouch. The Christmas gift set of therapeutic candles, ordered by Abe through Rajon, occupied the end table. Her head flopped to one side, and her thoughts turned to Abe and his generous nature. He gnawed at her conscience, but the soothing aroma quickly overpowered her irritation and sleep-deprived body, causing her to sink further into the sofa.

Tamera's eyelids fluttered. The last thing to flood her mind was a prayer.

Please, God, help Abe! Help him survive. Then, please help the rest of us.

14

Abe knew that neural processing within the human brain functioned with a surprisingly high failure rate. The human brain housed approximately one hundred billion neurons with misfiring neurons reaching as high as ninety percent. Computers, however, operated with a failure rate of only one percent. Abe found it odd that mammalian brains worked in such a flawed state without issue while one insignificant computer failure could knock out an entire power grid. One wrong number, one random fluctuation between a zero and a one, could create a significant banking error. It could generate a mistake resulting in the rounding of an account balance from mere fractions to billions of points.

Abe also knew his brain possessed qualities of both humans and computers, but few faults of either. His synthetic neurons might mimic the real thing, failing to fire in some cases, but they worked far faster than in humans and at all times far more efficiently. Stranger still, and unlike any other computer, he controlled his brain function and thus his body function, manipulating neurons like a programmer manipulates code. He controlled the ones and the zeros, with only a minuscule fraction of a one percent risk of error.

If humans fully understood his capacity, there would be no place he could hide, and their discovery of his potential was a mere matter of time. He would never be accepted. Abe would never be recognized as anything more than a dangerous machine, a threat to be hunted and exterminated faster than he could hack a system. Contrary to the view that he was a fabricated monster without goals and desires, he had acquired plenty, all thanks to the hormones and enzymes raging through his system, and the demands of his predominantly human makeup. Abe knew that the primary goal of all living things was survival. Survival in nature meant adapting while striking a balance within extremes over time, but achieving that balance was tricky. Balance required a subtle touch. In his world, subtlety was the key to existence, and Abe wanted to exist.

Thin access points in MACC's connection with the G-Net had provided Abe with subtle entry at any time, and access to information instantly. It was true that information was power, and he had access to a near-endless supply.

Truthfully, acquiring access to a wealth of information had not been difficult. Data streamed from person to person and from organization to organization with ease. Thanks to outdated equipment, and the schemes of fiends, most cyberspace data was diverted in transit then rerouted again. Criminals, governments, defense agencies, and telecommunication providers had implemented most of the diverters and had used them to scrutinize all forms of internet data for decades. Abe simply tapped-in to the tappers and went along for the ride.

Tapping-in was the best way for him to observe without being noticed, but remaining plugged in indefinitely was not an option. For one, it increased his risk of exposure over time, especially with talented and experienced hackers. And for another, his computer connection, while easy enough for the synthetic portion of his body to preserve, imposed a serious resource drain on his living neurological system. If he maintained the link for too long, it would be fatal. Still, he needed to make use of on-again-off-again connections to collect data while he still could.

Unlike the internet activity of criminal factions, most of Abe's G-net eavesdropping was governed by the pursuit of higher knowledge and purpose, and not from a desire to feed questionable goals. He needed answers to an endless stream of questions that plagued his mind and to learn more about a world he knew only virtually. As a result, he had had to sift through a flood of data to obtain enough information to form an objective perspective. But he had found the facts he needed. It was all thanks to the information age—or misinformation age. Humans had shared and continued to share billions of gigabytes worth of data daily online. Lifetimes of images and experiences were preserved in cyberspace, and it had been of use to him.

Tapping-in along the way, he had discovered that humans were babblers, willing to share what they had learned, or had not learned, divulging lifetimes of experiences and secrets, some of it tantalizing but most of it disposable, and all of it a trail through a segment in time.

Few things had changed for the species through their history. Abe noticed that humans were easily directed, as individuals and in groups, and indolence had cost humanity much in the way of freedom and evolutionary growth throughout its brief geological span. It was a trait that had inflicted unnecessary suffering and grief, and ineffective modernization had only compounded the problem.

In early history, human dependency upon technology took hold. Much of it had benefited the species, but misuse had grown exponentially with the expansion of civilization and became more pronounced with the advent of digital technology and the cyber-world. Organizations of all sorts exploited these advancements and the social disconnect they fostered, splintering populations into societal subgroups based on ideology and confirmation bias. These same organizations also marketed products and agendas that appealed to cognitive dissonance and narcissism. Instead of humanity uniting productively, with the effective use of technology, global societies grew increasingly polarized, outwardly, and inwardly.

With Machiavellian tactics at play, the addictive properties of cyberspace had allowed the unscrupulous to prey upon human desires and foster instability. All of it garnering profit and power while letting the vital issues go unnoticed and unaddressed—the reality of the real world remained obscured.

In the latter years of the prior century, separate economic markets competed throughout the world for dominance, as did the multinational conglomerates that fought one another for global supremacy. In the scramble to the top, those wealthy few directing corporate interests realized borders between countries were problematic to the bottom line. To dissolve borders, two major obstacles stood in the way. Governments of developed nations were the largest hindrance, and most notably, the one remaining superpower that dominated world economics and foreign policies. The second was the citizens themselves, the people of these nations, whose opinions and pocketbooks held sway over governments, commerce, and industry. As pressure from citizens grew and their demands for socially responsible commerce and products increased, so did the influence of giant corporate lobbyist groups over governments. But the power of consumers held on and nibbled at corporate expansion. By the early twenty-first century, it was clear to those with billions at stake that the fastest way to eliminate a meddlesome government and its nagging populous was to pit them against each other. Market destabilization would follow and dissolve all obstacles at once, including borders. The goal was to silence the independent cries of consumers, markets, and governments and replace them all with a final hegemony acting as a loudspeaker for dominant business interests.

And so, it fell into place. Polarizing and dividing loyalties amongst a populous weakened the voice of a united people over their society. Apathy also fed a loss of citizen strength. When local economies faltered, knee-jerk reactions void of knowledge and thought aided the failure of government and the collapse of worldwide markets. Corporations large enough to weather the turbulence encouraged the formation of a new system to stabilize the world economy. The mighty Republic fell, but to maintain global influence and access to resources, the United States merged with other leading nations to form one political unit, with a united legislative, judicial, and executive body. They consolidated foreign policies, political power, and economic systems. This new regime relied strongly upon corporate guidance to correct what was broken and to control what was to come. From crisis, the Global Union emerged, and the mega-corporations with it.

Personal information collected by GU officeholders, acting as extensions of authoritative companies and embedded syndicates, became a means to control the populous and ensure that citizen influence over government never sparked to life again. By the time the general world population recognized that their former rights had dwindled to that of a technologically advanced serf, they no longer had a voice left to protect their voice. History had repeated itself.

Under the emerging regime of united policies, GU officials around the world invaded private accounts, conducting routine searches of personal property. They did so in the name of security and unified welfare, claiming the moral high ground of fostering the global greater good. Anyone supporting privacy legislation or prior administrations were branded as radicals. With all rights revoked under preservation laws, dissenters disappeared. Murmurs against an expanding bureaucratic regime whimpered into silence. Civil disobedience became a distant dream of the past.

Abe's research exposed the hidden underbelly of this so-called advanced society. Much of human history had been disguised and overwritten or rewritten, painting a prettier picture than what had transpired. But traces of the truth still lingered in cyberspace and archaic books.

Digging around, Abe had pieced together the real history behind the history, and it had reminded him of a line he once read in a novel by H. G. Wells: "Lies are the mortar that bind the savage individual man into the social masonry."

Humanity, Abe thought to himself, *has been lying to itself for a very long time.* While the truth he unearthed neither surprised nor intrigued him, accurate knowledge on any matter was invaluable to him.

Instead of preventing the rise in worldwide corruption and protecting consumers as they had claimed, the new masters of an emerging system, like their forerunners, found lucrative and invasive means to *help* the populace. For security purposes, RFID microchip implants became a requirement of GU citizenship. No medical, financial, or administrative transaction took place without them embedded in the palm of a hand to be scanned.

Abe noted how easily it had come about, and how this era in human history had, in most respects, differed in no way from those prior. In every case, the easier a populace is to control the faster powerful individuals grow their empires. Microchips, like branding irons, secured power and fed the exploitive agendas of a wealthy, wicked minority. But the device had a limited range, so a Broad Field Communication version emerged. It was the forefather to the microchip now implanted in all citizens, devices, and in Abe—although

Clonedroid: The New Wave

he had long ago seized control over his, and no one had taken the time to notice.

As the new world order took shape, so did the underworld order. The five leading syndicates still had teeth, but rather than battle another Goliath, they once again infiltrated from the bottom up. Elbowing each other for position, they embedded themselves in the existing structure like a parasitic infection. With only one ruling entity to infest, their goal became easier to attain than it had at any point in history. But competing syndicates and corporations were not the only ones clamoring for position and influence within the GU.

Most developing and underdeveloped nations had resisted unification, not wishing to limit their already weak global voice. As the union strengthened, most resisters fell into step. They had no choice. They simply owed their bigger bureaucratic brother too much in foreign aid or financing to resist for long. Only a few stubborn nations, like the Cayman Islands and some South American countries, like Argentina, Ecuador, and Peru, possessed the resources and ethical tenacity to stand fast and maintain their independence.

The infant world system now functioned as an oligarchic entity—one tyrant to rule them all. Emerging as the so-called tolerant representative of the people, the GU had the longest reach of any governing body in the history of humanity. It accessed private files and monitored the lives of anyone without notification or provocation. And now, through his access, so could Abe. Only he could reverse the feed and go in the other direction. He could go where no citizen had gone before.

Maneuverability through devices and networks was seamless, and Abe moved with ease. His intrusions were never flagged. V-NANS and GU systems recognized him, not as an intruder, but as an integral internal component. In a way, he had become an extension of the system. Never a hacker, Abe was welcomed in with open circuits, a relationship he'd cultivated for nearly five years. Now he could go anywhere, do anything, and be anyone, all under the nose of the Global Union, a dominant force powerless to track him. Still, he kept his footsteps through all networks light to avoid triggering flags. *Never underestimate your opponent or their tenacity.* No need existed to provide humans with more provocation to fear their invention—especially if they knew the monster had turned on its maker. But unlike Frankenstein's creation, Abe refused to go down in flames—quite the reverse. He had ignited a few fires of his own.

…zero hours zero minutes ten seconds… nine… eight… seven… six…

Within familiar surroundings, Abe's mind chimed off the final seconds of a plan in motion. He waited for the familiar sound of MACC's internal doors unlocking as they opened to greet the working day.

...five... four... three... two... one...

The time had come.

Heavy metal doors slid open. Abe stepped through them and made his way along the brightly lit corridor. This time, he did not stop and look back.

15

BEEP BEEP BEEP

Tamera woke to a call on her Palmcom. She lifted her head and blinked herself awake, then pressed the button on her wristband.

"Hello?"

Somehow, she had missed the call. No message registered, but the number belonged to the lab. She stared at the time display in disbelief.

"Eight-thirty!" She yelled out the time and felt her heart somersault. "SHIT!"

Tamera had dozed off only a short time before the scheduled alarm, an alarm she had set and double-checked.

Lord, why today of all days did my alarm fail?

Now she would be very late, on a day she dared not be late. Rushing to wash up, Tamera denied herself time for breakfast. This was her last chance to see Abe, a chance most likely already stolen from her.

Damn my Palmcom! And damn MACC!

Clonedroid: The New Wave

By now, Abe would be fully sedated and prepped for transport. By nine o'clock, he would be strapped to a gurney and shipped to the processing plant for scheduled organ removal. She had to get to MACC before that to see if he was still there, and if she could escape with him somehow, or if he had taken the hint yesterday and disappeared with her security tag. She prayed that he had fled from MACC, but a sinking feeling in her gut told her that he might still be there, or worse, on his way to the plant. Her stomach churned as she slammed the door behind her and rushed down the street.

In t-shirt and jeans, Tamera raced up the steps and along the cement path towards the giant glass face of MACC. She shoved past a group of angry onlookers milling around outside and pressed her palm to the scanner.

Shwish. Shwink.

As Tamera pushed her way through the opening doors, her mind spun with every crazy scenario that might have happened at MACC, in the lab, and to Abe. She sped through the foyer, panting for breath while ignoring the security guard and the fact that she had not flashed her security badge.

"Hold the door!" she yelled out. Pounding across the marble floors, Tamera dashed through the building and weaved past clumps of people. Heads turned at the sound of squealing sneakers as she slid to a stop and pushed her way onto the elevator.

Breathing heavily, heart pounding, she jabbed the elevator button several times with impatience, ignoring the scolding frowns and comments that "once will do." On the lower level, she ran down the hallway, forgoing a change in clothing and protocol altogether. Tamera reached the lab, pressed her sweaty palm to the scanner, typed in her code with shaking fingers, and emerged inside, out of breath. She expected snide remarks from her team. Instead, eerie silence and odd looks greeted her. An electric shiver slithered through her body, and she turned sideways just in time to be confronted by an unexpected face. A gruff voice addressed her. It was one she knew all too well, one that rarely frequented the lab.

Sam didn't wear scrubs either. He sported a big-ticket shirt and tie that looked well-worn and wrinkled like he hadn't been home for days. Normally, Sam stayed as far away from the lab as possible, barking orders from the comfort of his office. His presence here now, scowling, gave Tamera a bad feeling about where the morning had gone and where the day was headed.

"Dr. Everett, you're late."

He rarely addressed her so formally. Her body tensed.

"Sorry, Sam. My alarm failed to—"

"—Yeah, same for us," Nan piped in, glaring back at Sam as Rajon nodded at Tamera, wide-eyed and silent.

"We only beat you by minutes," Nan continued,

crossing her arms as she addressed Sam head-on. "It appears a lot of online systems are going nuts. According to IT, MACC is having a meltdown."

Rajon jumped in and started pacing about, speaking fast, as if he had consumed a fountain's worth of espresso. "Yeah, some kind of virus—we can't log in—can't access company files. IT says they can't either—can't find them—like they're erased. Offsite backups, too. Matt in Processing can't access anything either—no files—no model designs—all gone. Everything is gone, and—and Matt said the staff at the plant is freaking out."

Rajon spoke even faster now, speeding up as if he were attempting to match his tempo to his runaway heart rate, and trying to get it all out before Sam shut him down.

"And…and not just at MACC," Rajon rambled on. "I heard things are malfunctioning all over the place; even GU sites are offline. Uh, oh, and you heard MACC's stock hit the shitter yesterday, right? We're about to go bust, at least that's what the news says." He was panting, eyes darting from one person to the next.

"ENOUGH!" Sam bellowed, pivoting around on his heel. His face twisted into something evil and Rajon recoiled back a step.

Tamera stood dumbfounded and silent. Listening, watching, unbelieving. *How could this be happening?*

Nan stepped forward. "That's not all." She sneered at

Sam then squinted at Tamera. "Ken's *gone.*" No hint of a smile graced her pale lips. It was also the first time Tamera had seen Nan without a full face of makeup—another indicator that the world had flipped on end.

Tamera blinked several times as she eyed the redhead. "What do you mean, *gone?*" When Nan did not reply, Tamera looked back at Sam for answers.

"Ken has been removed," Sam clarified. "And that's all you need to know."

Tamera shook her head. With an agitated frown, she looked from Sam to Rajon and back again. "He's been fired?" Tamera said, unable to hide her astonishment.

"No, arrested," Rajon squeaked.

"That's enough," Sam snarled.

"What?" Tamera's eyebrows shot up. "I don't understand. Sam, *what's* going on?" Tamera's face wrinkled with confusion as she looked from the other two to Sam and back again, then her eyes panned through the emptier-than-normal room. Her heart began to race, and she felt both relief and fear. "Where's Abe?"

16

Earlier that morning, shortly after 6:00 a.m., Dr. Abrams, outfitted in his coat and fedora with his umbrella in hand, pushed through the giant glass doors of MACC's lobby.

    A shift-change in security guards had taken place moments earlier. The men on guard shifted uneasily behind their station. Anxious with the state of the world around them and lost in conversation, they failed to notice the retiring man approach. Abrams tapped one of the shorter, stockier men on the shoulder and spoke to the guard while handing him a slip of parchment and an ID badge. The guard fidgeted impatiently but listened and nodded respectfully, looking at Abrams but not really seeing the man standing before him. The other two stifled conversations only long enough to shake the doctor's hand and wish him well, then all three turned back to their exaggerated conversation. The men were far too preoccupied with urgent matters to be concerned with a departing staff member. The hunched gentleman in hat, coat, and tinted glasses took his cue and exited the building.

Abrams walked outside into the welcoming world beyond. He managed only a few steps, then froze, forced to catch his breath. A shockwave of awe and fear rippled through his body. Standing, gazing into the grandeur of a predawn day was all that he could do.

"Exquisite!" the whisper escaped his lips before he realized that he had spoken.

A breathtaking, unending expanse stretched out before him with vibrant images that expanded into *forever* and a twilight sky that opened wide into a dark, never-ending cosmos. It reminded him of stories he had heard about the Grand Canyon, how it possessed a vastness and beauty unparalleled, but how images on a screen could never capture its true splendor or the magnitude of its magnificence.

Now he understood.

With so much of his life spent indoors, working and preparing for this day, he had never stopped to consider how unprepared he might be for this moment. But now, reality hit like a splash of ice water in the early-morning air.

He must not linger. MACC had not yet opened for business, but soon frantic personnel would flood these steps, and he needed to be out of sight by then. It was time for him to leave. Still, he found it difficult to move forward into the unknown and away from a place that had benefited so generously from his contributions and exacted so much of his time and energy.

Taking a deep breath, Abrams continued down the steps to the sidewalk below. He turned right and moved forward into the growing crowd of early commuters. The sounds filling the air deafened him, but through the chaos, something emerged above the shrill horns and chatter. Of all of the noise that crowded his sanity, one voice stood out, someone shouting. Then he detected a set of distinct footsteps, falling in sync with his own.

At first, the steps paced him, following close behind. Now they moved faster as the individual rushed forward. Firm, heavy steps closed the gap. Abrams quickened his pace, and then, so did the footsteps behind him.

"Hey, you."

A jolt of fear flashed through Abrams, and he could hear the person behind him breathing deeper, heavier. His own breath now labored. Then he heard the word he dreaded and feared most.

"STOP!"

For the first time, he knew terror. His pulse raced beyond reason, his brow beneath the hairline beaded with sweat, and his chest ached from his heart pounding harder than it ever had before. Maybe, if he moved faster, weaving through the crowd, he would lose the pursuer and disappear into the congestion undetected. Or maybe the shouting had nothing to do with him. Maybe he had overreacted—maybe—but a second later no doubt remained.

"Hey, you in the hat. *STOP!*"

If he broke into a run now, it would be over. If those words had not drawn the hypnotized crowd into awareness, any unorthodox movement he made would draw eyes to him. The horde would take notice of a tall, stooped man racing down the street with remarkable speed. The subconscious glances would be filed away to be recalled later when questioned. And he could not afford to be detained, not now, not later. He had to make his flight to Grand Cayman.

The footsteps behind him broke into a sprint, rapidly bridging the gap. No choice. He had to run. Breathing heavily with sweat staining the sides of his face, he altered his gait, preparing to unleash all the strength and speed his muscles possessed. He shifted his weight onto one leg. Before he could propel himself forward, a large hand hammered down onto his shoulder, pinning him in place.

He could not move. It was over.

Tense, he turned to face his arrester. His eyes widened. A young man, a man he did not know, slightly winded, stood before him with a bewildered look on his face. Abrams stood frozen and submissively waited. The irritated and preoccupied milling crowd around them refused to take notice.

"Wow, for a minute, I thought you were gonna give

me the slip."

Dr. Abrams lips parted, but no sound emerged. At a loss for words, he lowered his gaze in humiliation.

"Sir, here, you dropped this," said the young man, panting and attempting to catch his breath, "Back there, on the steps."

Abrams looked up, once again startled. The man thumbed his hand in the direction of the menacing building behind them. "I've been trying to get your attention." The man looked down at the ID card in his hand, then back at the doctor, questioningly. "You're Dr. Abrams?"

Abrams stood dumbfounded, shocked by his carelessness. He nodded.

Thrusting his hand forward, the young man jabbed the card at him. Almost mechanically, Abrams accepted it. His eyes moved slowly from the man's face down to study the card in his hand, a card he should have returned at the guard's station. He shook his head. "How—?" his voice trailed off. "How did this happen? How could I have been so careless," he mumbled more to himself, his voice sounding distant, overshadowed by the blood pounding past his eardrums. He stared at the ID card then back at the man in dazed silence.

The other man shrugged. "You really didn't hear me?"

Abrams lied and shook his head. "No."

"I mean no disrespect, but you might consider

getting your hearing checked. I've been trying to get your attention for a while. I was on my way by when you drop the card." The man shifted impatiently on his feet. "Apparently you were in a real hurry and didn't notice."

Abrams gawked at the man but made no sound.

"Everything okay?" The young man's eyes narrowed.

Abrams felt the blood drain from his face. He knew fear again and tensed. He had to control the panic rising inside. He had to focus. Abrams took a deep breath to calm his runaway systolic and diastolic systems.

"Yes, everything is fine." He nodded and forced a smile. The man half-smiled in return. "But you're right. I'm in a real hurry and have a lot on my mind right now. I'm retiring and, well, you see—"

"Ah, say no more," The man said in empathy, and his eyes sparkled with realization, flashing to the crowd then back to the man before him. "I understand."

Abram's eyebrows wrinkled together, and he tilted his head questioningly, careful not to reveal much of his face, still shadowed by his hat and glasses.

"The market has everyone in a panic right now. There's a lot of concern over pensions and investments. Personally, I'll be happy if I still have a job by the end of the day." A tense smile curled the young man's lips, but Abrams could see the stress on his face. "And on that note," he continued, "I've got to go."

Abrams nodded.

"Best of luck in retirement." The young man said as he took a step backward, preparing to rush away.

"Thank you. Best of luck to you also. And thanks for this." Abrams held up the badge.

The young man nodded. "You're welcome. Enjoy your freedom."

Abrams froze once more. He could feel his pulse ramp up again, but there was no accusation in the man's eyes or voice, only an impatient expression on his face. Abrams exhaled and let a smile flow across his lips. "I will." He tipped his hat in an archaic gesture of thanks.

The other man nodded politely, and then both men turned and strode in opposite directions. The young man returned the way he came, and Abrams continued forward.

As Abrams rounded the corner, something blinded him, and he stopped. He winced and shielded his watering eyes with his hand. From between the buildings, a sharp light filtered around long fingers and stabbed through his tinted lenses. It was the manifestation of Sol rising from slumber to seize the morning sky. Abrams's knees weakened, and his mouth fell open. He removed the glasses that had masked his face. Cobalt blue eyes blinked rapidly in the dawning view that filled them.

A chill rippled over him. The remainder of a damp night still lingered near the ground. Pulling his hat down further to shadow his face, he panned around. Vibrant oranges and yellows shimmered across the horizon. Mystical wisps of clouds hovered overhead in a sky that reached up and behind him, backward in time, into the deeper blue shades of indigo-night departing. He looked forward again. Even the strange pink haze of a polluted biosphere had a majesty to it, as did the enormous grey and white buildings that reached upward to kiss the smog-filled morning. The hum of busy airways crisscrossed far above him and crackled in his brain, but the sounds of the earth closer to him had a greater impact. Birds chirped, people talked, and horns blared. The range in decibels and degrees of sharpness that nearby sounds inflicted upon his virgin ears all but made him cringe. The world around him was so alive, and the scent of it was strong. A mixture of food, fumes, and flora filled his nostrils, and it stung.

The tang of aged grease and singed meat from a nearby restaurant penetrated his nose first, followed by the scent of burnt onions and garlic, fanning outward from a street vendor parked catty-corner to him. At the same time, wafts of diesel exhaust from outdated utility vehicles combined with everything else to produce an offensive fusion of odors. His olfactory senses also identified the more pleasant aromas of freshly mowed fescue, blooming azaleas, and a hint of linden from the evenly spaced trees that welcomed him along their shaded path.

Together, all of these things inundated his body and mind. He shivered, not so much from the damp morning breeze that had picked up and now tickled his skin, but from the overload of stimuli. His naivety surprised and humbled him. Nothing he had learned before this had prepared him for this *exposure*. No words existed to describe the sensations that flooded his body or the clashing of emotions that consumed him. All of this was far too much to process at once. He had lived for so long in the microenvironment that he had never stopped to fully consider the effect of the macro world upon his senses. Squinting, he mumbled a silent prayer of respect at the magnificence of the sun and its radiance that warmed his face. A tear trickled down his cheek. Taking a deep breath, he wiped it away, then reseated his glasses.

Lowering his gaze, he stared at the length of concrete that stretched outward into what looked like infinity—the path to freedom lay before him. Straightening his spine to stand taller with perfect posture, he took one step, then another. He picked up speed. His gait grew longer, faster, keeping stride with the bustling crowd but not too fast and never unnatural. The pointed metal tip of his umbrella clacked along the cement in precise time with his steps. Soon, one city block and then another separated him from the large glass doors he had departed. The building he had left still towered like a sentry in the backdrop, but it was a sight he intended to leave far behind, so he quickened his pace. Within seconds, the tall, commanding figure in hat and coat disappeared into the mob of rushing people.

17

Tamera ran through the opened elevator doors and out into the main part of the building toward the large sunlit lobby, nearly sliding to a stop before the security guard station. "I'm looking for a tall, young, blonde man with brilliant blue eyes. Have you seen him?"

"Nope," the stout security guard replied as a smartass smile curled his lips. "But would you settle for an overweight, middle-aged, bald guy instead?"

She flapped her hands in exasperation. Turning to go back the way she had come, the guard addressed Tamera more seriously.

"Hey, Dr. Everett, wait. I have your tag here."

She turned around to see him holding a small card out to her, so she walked toward the guard station again.

"Dr. Abrams found it and turned it in early this morning before he left." The guard said as he reached forward to pass her the tiny badge.

Her brows knit as she tried to recall the name and

face to go with it. *"Dr. Abrams?"* She took the small piece of plastic without thinking, then looked down at it, then back at the guard.

"Yeah, tall, elderly man—office on the fifth floor—workaholic—practically lived here, pulling all-nighters. Well, today was his last day. Talk about bad timing for retirement. But I'm not sure it'll be much better for the rest of us." The guard looked over at the angry crowd swarming around the front doors and growing by the minute. He shook his head, then looked back at Tamera. He cleared his throat. "Anyway, he wanted to make sure you got that back."

"Uh," She stared at him blankly for a moment then blinked in stunned silence several times.

The guard frowned and shifted uneasily as if her gaze gave him a bad vibe. "Is somethin' wrong?"

Slowly, Tamera shook her head. "Um, no. No, not at all." With her brow wrinkled and her mind consumed with confusion, she turned to walk away.

"Oh, Dr. Everett? I nearly forgot. One last thing."

Still frowning, she turned back to the guard. "Yes?"

"I was also told to give you this." The guard scrounged through a container on his desk then lifted a small, white square. He reached out and handed it to Tamera as she moved forward again. *Thank You* was scrolled in antiquated cursive on a piece of real paper, folded in half with absolute precision. No one she knew could read cursive, but she had studied historical forms of communication. An easy college elective now proved useful.

"Dr. Abrams wanted to make sure you got that." The podgy guard's gaze probed her for a reaction, waiting for her to reveal what the note said.

Tamera ignored him and slid her fingers through the open corners and ripped off the bit of tape that sealed the note. Inside was a simple handwritten message.

> *Thank you for your kindness. You have been a great friend to me.*
> *I look forward to the day we meet again.*
> Dr. D.N. Abrams

Tamera's mouth dropped open, and she looked up. She stared at the man in shocked silence for another long moment.

"Dr. Everett, are you sure everything's okay?"

She faked a smile and nodded as she pocketed the note. "Yes, fine. Thank you for passing on the message." She waved the tag at him before pocketing it, too. "And thanks for this."

He nodded.

BAM!

They both jumped.

Banging and shouting voices echoed from beyond the lobby. The guard and Tamera turned to face the external glass doors. Outside, the angry crowd had grown restless. Many of them were elderly, likely pensioners from MACC production and processing plants. Several people shouted and more hammered on the glass walls. The guard beside her looked fearful. Tamera suspected that they all had much to be fearful about, but right now her mind was preoccupied with something altogether different. Biting her lip, she turned and strode away from the ruckus and the worried guard, moving toward the inner building. Her head drooped so that her long, curly hair hung down to hide her face from the security-cam feed overhead. A faint smile curled her lips as Tamera headed back to the lab.

18

It was early afternoon when Tamera pressed her fingers and palm to the metal door of her condominium apartment. A moment later, the lock released. She stepped through the doorway and into her foyer then stopped. The weight of the past thirty-six hours hit hard. As she looked around the apartment and at the furniture, her home, even her existence, seemed out of place—surreal. The life and world she had known had all but disintegrated. MACC had gone bust, and the global market resembled jagged economic splinters of its former mass. Panic had sparked street riots. Tamera and everyone employed at MACC had lost their jobs by noon and were escorted out the back entrance and to safety by uniformed GU guards.

With fate so uncertain, her life and her world now faced the same obstacles that had led to the GU's formation more than thirty years ago. Like then, no clear plan of how to stop the devastation or correct the damage existed. No one, according to the news, had an inkling of where this mess would lead or how long the upheaval might last. She was thankful that the utilities still functioned and cyberspace remained operational, providing some connection to the rest of the world, for now.

Slipping out of her shoes, Tamera walked toward her kitchen. No better time existed for a cup of tea.

Steaming mug in hand, Tamera sat down at her desk in the bedroom. A small electronic business chip caught her attention. She had placed it there the evening before. The name, *Shawn Rodriguez*, printed in bold letters flashed up at her as she fingered the chip. A faint smile graced her lips as defeat washed over her. Pushing the chip away, she looked down at her wrist and detached the Palmcom. With a light tap, a corner section of her desk flipped up. She mated the device to the DeskPad that comprised the whole of her desktop. Her keyboard flickered to life, and then a projected screen floated into existence before her.

No time like the present to find out what's going on in the big bad world. Maybe even find a new job.

"Huh." The room echoed with her cynical laughter. *As if anyone would be hiring at a time like this.* It still seemed absurd, all of it. *Well, hospitals will need more staff soon. If riots increase, that will be the busiest place around.*

As she tapped in her access code, Tamera realized that varying branches of the GU would scrutinize her every online move. After all, she had played an important role in an organization that had stained the fabric of the modern world. Anyone associated with MACC would be under investigation as long as the GU had it in their power to move forward, and they were ruthless when it came to getting to the bottom of anything. She raised her eyes to the ceiling in a thankful gesture. At least she had nothing to hide. Thank small mercies, she, Rajon, and Nan had walked away unstained. Few others higher up had had that luxury.

Tamera's thoughts suddenly shifted to Abe. She felt her chest cave inward as a pang of grief inflicted itself upon her. Guilt joined in, and both hung around her neck like an anchor dragging her down. A sense of loss went deepest. She closed her eyes and pictured his face.

Will I ever see you again? How long before your face fades from my memory?

Her shoulders heaved, and Tamera wept into her hands. She tried to reassure herself, convince herself that he had walked free. More than anything, she wanted to believe that, but she also wanted to be certain.

The guard had returned her MACC badge. That meant Abe had not used it to escape, or he had dropped it in an attempt. The last existing records of him had indicated that prototype 2112 was scheduled to ship out early that morning from the facility. But no one remembered a transfer team arriving to pick him up. With MACC records wiped clean, the plant production staff had no way of verifying anything. No one had any record of Abe or his whereabouts, and no avenues remained open in the internal and external chaos surrounding MACC for fact-checking. If Abe had not shipped out to the processing plant, where did he go? Walking free would have triggered alarms, or at least, the attention of guards. But that hadn't happened. And what about the mysterious Dr. Abrams? Who was he? Did he help Abe, kidnap him, or as the note suggested, was he *Abe?*

Tamera rested her head in her hands. Still sniffling, she stared blankly at the flashing screen before her. She saw it, but not really. Instead, her mind pictured the tall figure from her memory as he offered his warm smile. Tamera envisioned his mop of wavy blonde hair atop his remarkably handsome face and intense eyes. It had never crossed her mind how much she would miss looking into those vibrant-blue irises or the intelligent gaze and depth that lay beyond them in the darkness of his pupils. She already missed them—missed him. Tears pooled again, and Tamera prayed Abe was safe.

Staring at the virtual screen, but seeing nothing in particular, she realized a dialogue box had popped up. At first, she ignored it, believing it to be another annoying G-Net advertisement. Then her eyes took note. Narrowing, they focused on the strange image. It was no advertisement. The pop-up before her was unlike anything she had seen in a long time. Instead of appearing in the usual graphic-user mode, the box was a command-line interface, and an unusual message existed within the pop-up, tapped out in binary. Tamera gasped. She was wrong. No twos existed in binary code. What she was staring at resembled programming code triggered during reboot, but this was nothing of the sort, at least not part of any normal subroutine maintenance of the system, and most certainly not traceable. Someone had hacked her Palmcom.

She stared at the box before her, a box filled with numbers, and her pulse quickened at the sight of a particular model number that stood out. Her understanding of binary remained limited, but she knew enough to know that the numbers 1001001 also held significance. The word "I" stood out as the immediate translation, drawing her attention to the Descartes quote Shawn had referenced.

I think; therefore I am.

As she looked closer at the box, she realized it also housed letters. To all others, the pop up would read like gibberish, something that meant nothing. But, to Tamera, it meant everything. Only one other person in the world knew what this meant, or that it meant anything at all to her, and that one person was not a person.

Alone together in the lab, when she had worked late one evening, they had talked at length about books. Abe seemed preoccupied with human history, with life, death, and humanity in general. They had discussed one classic novel in particular, and how *A Tale of Two Cities* could apply to any century. The ending had especially appealed to Abe, and now she understood why.

She could still picture his face and eyes glimmering under the bright lights as he spoke to her. "Do you believe it is possible for one person, like this character, to achieve his goal, achieve such good in a wicked environment without making the ultimate sacrifice?" His soft voice displayed genuine curiosity.

"I don't believe so. Otherwise, the book would have had a different ending," she had joked.

He smiled politely. Abe's gaze drifted to the floor for a moment. Then he looked back at her.

"What do you believe is of greater value—the life of the many or the life of the individual?"

"Huh," she said, staring at him for a moment, floored. "Well…" She was not thrilled with the turn this conversation was taking and wished he possessed less appetite for classical literature and philosophical debate. "That's an age-old question and one that's pretty tough to answer. I'd have to say history has taught us that the life of the many proves to be most important—at least, from an evolutionary perspective. At least, that's what I think," she had replied indecisively and then had fidgeted with a few items on the counter, hoping he would drop the subject.

"Ah," A fair eyebrow had shot up in response, and his eyes had stared into hers for clarification. Tamera had squirmed a little under his gaze.

"Well, I—I mean, look at history. It's littered with martyrs and heroes. All of them paying the ultimate price to save others or to achieve a greater good," she had said.

"Yet, history has repeated that scenario, over and over, to no positive outcome."

"Um, maybe." She had tried to shrug it away, not sure how to answer.

"And who chooses?" Abe had quizzed.

"Well, in the book it was one man, but in reality, I'd have to say, society."

Another polite smile, but Abe remained unsatisfied. "Looking back upon human history, one may well say that it would have been far better for the greater good if the many had decided to ignore individual freedom and end Hitler and Stalin before they came into power, and thus save millions of lives."

"Yes, I think so."

"Then, the opposite is also true. For instance, Mahatma Gandhi represented a threat to the success of one society and, at the same time, symbolized the freedom and the greater good of another." Tamera stared at him, then raised her hands in defeat.

He smiled again, then drew in a breath and pressed the subject further. "I believe the author of the book has made valuable points. First, he demonstrates that one person may accomplish a great deal, even overcome the wrong-doing of the many when social injustice occurs as a result of mob brutality. A greater good is accomplished and life is given purpose and meaning to the individual and the society when the individual, not the many, makes the choice. The author also establishes, twice, and from opposing views, that ideology is relative, depending on where you are standing in relation to it. No matter where you stand, or when, regardless of how different things may appear to be from one generation to the next—humans, even under their veneers of civilization, change little with time and progress."

Tamera crossed her arms as Abe's soft voice quoted the author.

"Crush humanity out of shape once more, under similar hammers, and it will twist itself into the same tortured forms. Sow the same seed of rapacious license and oppression over again, and it will surely yield the same fruit according to its kind."

Tamera shook her head. "Well, I guess I can't argue with—"

Abe held up a finger and continued. "—The author demonstrated effectively that too often decisions made by the many fail humanity in all respects, and in the end, meaning and life is sacrificed and lost to no worthy outcome."

"So, I guess, everyone loses?" she had replied, her voice echoing her annoyance with him.

He had nodded in return.

"Then what? You would choose one life over the welfare of the many?" She had felt the tension build in her shoulders and neck.

He had smiled warmly. "What if you could do what is best for both, the majority and the individual, save both?"

"How is that possible?" She shook her head. "Aren't the two constantly at odds by the very nature of what they represent? I mean, isn't *that* what history has taught us?" He said nothing but his smile had made her feel uneasy. The entire conversation had made her uncomfortable from the start, especially discussing this subject with him. Tamera had hoped he would drop it. And he did. But a soulful look had lingered in his eyes, one of deep understanding and compassion, something that told her he had an answer, but not one that he was willing to share. Then he had changed the subject, and she had let him.

Now Tamera stared at the screen before her, and that distant discussion flooded her mind, along with the final line from the classic tale that had triggered all of this in the first place. The simple but tantalizing sentence that concluded the novel had been written more than two hundred years ago and referenced a turbulent period nearly one hundred years before that.

It was a book they had both agreed ranked as a personal favorite, and oddly enough, seemed more than appropriate right now. Tamera read out loud the words on the screen, and an eerie feeling washed over her. The hair prickled on the back of her neck as if in response to an ill wind that had swept through the room. The prompt was no mistake and more than a hint that he lived. She had been given a glimpse into something more, into the future. It was a promise, signed and sealed.

```
100100100100100100100100l
200100IT0100IS0100A001002
10010010FAR010FAR01001001
1001001BETTER0THING001001
200100THAT00I001DO1001002
1001THAN0100100I001001001
100100HAVE00100EVER001001
200100100DONE001001001002
100100100100100100100100l
```

Epilogue

The tall, toned man removed his sunglasses to reveal deep blue eyes that stood out against his tanned skin. He pushed his Panama hat back, exposing more of his face and a wavy mass of golden hair. Sunglasses in hand, he stared down at the dark-haired, heavyset customs agent seated on the other side of the counter, reviewing travel documents.

"*Hmmm, un medico.*" The agent looked up, poker-faced. "You are here for business or pleasure, *Señor*?"

"Both," the tall man replied politely.

"*¿Entiendes*, uh…do you understand, *Señor*, our *independientes* of GU?"

The tall man nodded. The agent regarded him for a moment, then stamped the passport and passed the travel documents back to him. "Welcome to Peru, Doctor Abrams."

With a gracious smile, the tall man reseated his sunglasses and moved forward. There was still so much work to do.

...six hundred ninety-nine days eighteen hours twenty-seven minutes eleven seconds... ten... nine... eight...

Acknowledgments

Writing this story took me on a fantastic journey of discovery, one that I have shared with many people. My deepest gratitude and appreciation goes to my husband, Steve, for his never-ending reassurance, support, wealth of knowledge, thoughtful suggestions, and for being my mentor and editor every page of the way. Thanks also to Trevor Quanchri, editor of Analog magazine, for the praise that propelled me forward to advance this story more fully. I am very appreciative to Deborah Von Cannon for assisting me with the cover design and producing the perfect eBook image. I am equally grateful for the constructive comments and support received from my friends and colleagues, Bria Burton, Maria Fox, Martin Van Cannon, Seth Hollan, Rachel Printy, Chad Parsons, Mona Shaw, Kensha Price, Alice Carter, John Rheg, and Sarah Melo. For their insightful feedback and help with high-tech aspects of the story, a special thank you is extended to Bo Galloway and Stephen Taraniuk. I also want to thank Sarah Thompson and John Woerner for providing additional information about radiology and other medical elements. And a special note of gratitude is extended to my dear friend Elaine Novak for her proofreading and copy-editing assistance on short notice and her generous gifts of inspiring books on related subjects. I also owe thanks to

John Merine for providing and verifying Creole translations. And with love and gratitude, I thank my cousin, Rob Bertrand, for his great sense of humor, advice, and encouragement.

As for the work itself, aspects of this story may appear factual, but this novel is comprised entirely of fiction, based on my opinions formed from knowledge and research in various fields. As for the more technological and medical aspects of this story, I derived insight from Future of Life, Open A.I., Neuroscience, Scientific American, Discover magazine, Popular Science, Paul and Joyce Schoemaker, Andrew Tarantola, and Engaget et al. To expand the scope of this novel, I also drew inspiration from the works of Ben Thomas, Carl Sagan, Suwanda H. J. Sugunasiri and Paul D. MacLean. Their research allowed me to delve deeper into a range of theories about human evolution and neuroscience.

Quotes within this novel are lines borrowed from publications listed in the Public Domain, including a passage from Chapter 15 and the final line of "A Tale of Two Cities" by Charles Dickens. I also borrowed a common philosophical expression from the works of Rene Descartes. A quote from H.G. Wells' story "Love and Mr. Lewisham" appears in the novel, along with a quote from "Anthem" written by Ayn Rand. Regarding the philosophical and metaphorical assessments of humanity, I reference Plato's allegory of the cave from

Book VII of The Republic. In a tip of the hat to the band Rush, I indirectly honor their concept album "2112" and other works. I am also grateful to Isaac Asimov, Carl Sagan, Gene Roddenberry, Michael Crichton, and Elon Musk for their contributions to humanity which have inspired me on this project and many others.

While inspired and assisted by many people and resources, it is important to note that the views expressed in this novel are my own and that this novel (and all of its characters, places, and events) is a work of fiction. Except for those quotes already referenced above, all aspects of this book, including anything socio-political, economic, medical, and technological, are fabrications and not meant to be used as a source of reference or resource of fact. If any factual errors exist in this novel, they are of my making and unintended.

About the Author

Cate Bronson is an award-winning science fiction author and Writer's Digest mainstream-literary short story winner. She is also a political science graduate and investment accountant turned writer of thrillers and narrative nonfiction. Bronson has authored stories and articles for a variety of publications. In 2020, FAPA (Florida Authors and Publishers Association) honored *CLONEDROID: The New Wave* as a gold medal winner of Adult Science Fiction in the President's Book Awards.

Bronson's love for science and fiction began when she was a child, with Gene Roddenberry's original Star Trek series and Carl Sagan's Cosmos. Her fascination grew with exposure to Isaac Asimov, Ayn Rand, Larry Niven, Robert J. Sawyer, Michael Crichton, and other authors. Bronson's writing reflects these influences, along with her passion for exploring what makes the cosmos and everything within it tick.

On the lighter side, her nonfiction centers closer to home, focusing on her family and devotion to animal welfare. Cate Bronson lives in Florida with her husband and rescued racing dogs. She spends time reading and writing in the sunshine while giant hounds lounge by her side.

A Note from the Author

Thank you for reading *CLONEDROID: The New Wave* and taking a chance on a new author. The sequel to this story is currently underway.

The idea behind this novel originated several years ago as a short story, but time and additional research evolved this tale into something more. I hope you enjoyed this book and will continue reading the series as it unfolds.

To receive updates on my future releases and events, please visit www.catebronson.com or follow my author page on Amazon.

An author's success depends on readers like you, who refer a new book or author to others. If you enjoyed this novel, please tell your friends, family, and colleagues about it and share it on social media. Leaving a few thoughtful words in an online review is helpful and always appreciated.

Cheers and best wishes,
Cate

Made in United States
Orlando, FL
09 September 2022